Kate Fortune's

It's been so difficult staying behind the scenes and having to play dead while my family needs me.

I almost missed the birth of my granddaughter Caroline's little baby. But luckily my faithful friend Sterling helped me sneak into the nursery. What a precious bundle of joy! I'm so relieved that mother and baby are doing fine.

I'm also keeping a close eye on my granddaughter Rachel—I mean "Rocky." She was never like her glamorous twin, Allie. Rocky was always a tomboy, downplaying her looks, though she is quite a lovely girl. I've always encouraged and nurtured her adventurous spirit, which is why I left her my airplanes. Now she can finally have her own business and do what she loves best—flying. I just know she's going to soar in the wilds of Wyoming. Now, if only she could meet Mr. Right....

A LETTER FROM THE AUTHOR

Dear Reader,

I grew up with two brothers and a sister and an extended family of uncles and an aunt who were close enough in age to be siblings. So, being part of a large, involved family is as natural to me as breathing. We played and argued and watched out for each other as children, and nothing's really changed now that we're all adults— though we do argue a lot less! Naturally, I was thrilled when I was asked to write a book for the Fortune's Children series.

Writing Rocky's story turned out to be an added bonus because she and Allie are identical twins, and I, too, have an identical twin sister—Brenda. We're best friends and always have been. And yes, we still get asked if we're twins whenever we go out in public together. People will probably still be asking us that when we're eighty!

I also found Kate Fortune to be a fascinating character. I, too, had strong, spunky grandmothers who knew what they wanted out of life and went after it. One even joined the circus with my grandfather and traveled all over the country back in the thirties and forties. Neither of them ever flew off to the jungles of South America by themselves, but they might have if they'd been given the chance.

I hope you like *The Wolf and the Dove*. I loved working with the other authors and, like you, look forward to reading their books on the Fortune Family. Enjoy!

Linda Turner

The Wolf and the Dove

LINDA TURNER

Published by Silhouette Books

America's Publisher of Contemporary Romance

To my twin sister, Brenda Murray—
my best friend and partner in crime
who was there from the beginning

SILHOUETTE BOOKS

THE WOLF AND THE DOVE

Copyright © 1996 by Harlequin Books S.A.

ISBN 0-373-50181-1

Special thanks and acknowledgment to Linda Turner
for her contribution to the Fortune's Children series.

Removable book marker strip is covered under U.S. Reissue
Patent No. 34,759.

Printed in U.S.A.

LINDA TURNER

always knew she was going to be a writer—with the wonderful characters in her family, how could she be anything else? Her grandfather snuck her and her twin sister into a circus tent when she was eight, and her parents never came across a road they didn't want to explore. Consequently, life has always been a series of adventures to be savored to the fullest, which is why she worked for the FBI, spent a summer at a Boy Scout camp as a cook and longs to see the Pyramids in Egypt.

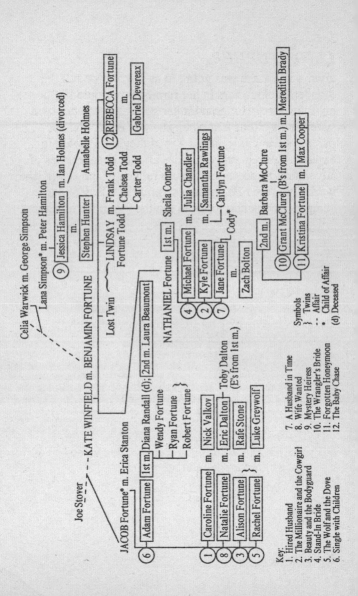

Celia Warwick m. George Simpson

Lana Simpson* m. Peter Hamilton

Joe Stover

-- KATE WINFIELD m. BENJAMIN FORTUNE

Jessica Hamilton m. Ian Holmes (divorced) (9)

Stephen Hunter

Annabelle Holmes

REBECCA Fortune (12)
m.
Gabriel Devereax

JACOB Fortune* m. Erica Stanton

Lost Twin
LINDSAY m. Frank Todd
Fortune Todd
Chelsea Todd
Carter Todd

NATHANIEL Fortune — 1st m. Sheila Conner

Michael Fortune (4) m. Julia Chandler

Kyle Fortune (2)
m. Samantha Rawlings
Caitlyn Fortune

Jane Fortune (7)
m.
Zach Bolton

Cody*

2nd m. Barbara McClure

Grant McClure (B's from 1st m.) m. Meredith Brady (10)

Kristina Fortune m. Max Cooper (11)

Adam Fortune (6) — 1st m. Diana Randall (d); 2nd m. Laura Beaumont

Wendy Fortune
Ryan Fortune }
Robert Fortune

Toby Dalton
(E's from 1st m.)

Caroline Fortune (1) m. Nick Valkov

Natalie Fortune (8) m. Eric Dalton

Alison Fortune (3) m. Rafe Stone

Rachel Fortune (5) m. Luke Greywolf

Symbols
} Twins
-- Affair
* Child of Affair
(d) Deceased

Key:
1. Hired Husband
2. The Millionaire and the Cowgirl
3. Beauty and the Bodyguard
4. Stand-In Bride
5. The Wolf and the Dove
6. Single with Children
7. A Husband in Time
8. Wife Wanted
9. Mystery Heiress
10. The Wrangler's Bride
11. Forgotten Honeymoon
12. The Baby Chase

FORTUNE'S Children

Meet the Fortunes—three generations of a family with a legacy of wealth, influence and power. As they unite to face an unknown enemy, shocking family secrets are revealed...and passionate new romances are ignited.

RACHEL "ROCKY" FORTUNE: The spirited beauty thrives on risks, so she ventures to the wilderness of Wyoming to start her own search-and-rescue business. But is she brave enough to take a chance on love?

LUKE GREYWOLF: The dedicated Native American doctor harbors a tragic secret and vows never to love again. But passionate Rachel arouses feelings too long denied....

MONICA MALONE: The legendary movie star is obsessed with revenge. She'll use seduction and blackmail to get her share of the Fortune empire... at any cost.

ADAM FORTUNE: Former military officer. He could keep order in the ranks, but he couldn't control his kids! Can this handsome single dad learn some lessons in fatherhood—and love?

LIZ JONES— CELEBRITY GOSSIP

Fellow gossips, here's the latest dirt on the Fortunes:

That *darling* Caroline and her sexy scientist husband announced the birth of their first child! Who would've thought this green-card marriage would end so joyously?

And Kyle reunited with an old flame and discovered he had a *love* child. I can't believe this city slicker is settling down on the Wyoming ranch for good. Ugh! All that dirt and grime...but of course I wouldn't mind a roll in the hay with a rugged cowboy!

But there's no gossip juicier than the scandalous break-up of Jake and Erica. Already my sources have spotted that louse with another woman. Poor Erica! If I were her, I'd go straight to the *La Dee Da Spa*, run up those credit cards at chic boutiques and forget all about that gorgeous hunk.... No wallowing in self-pity for me!

Well, I don't know about you, but I've got a feeling something big is about to happen with those unpredictable Fortunes....

One

With his usual enthusiasm, Michael Hawk gave Dr. Luke Greywolf a fierce hug, then ran out of the examining room as fast as his injured leg would allow, his attention jumping to the toy he would pick out at the nurses' station before he left with his mother. A muscle clenching in his square jaw, Luke watched the five-year-old awkwardly make his way down the hall and swore, long and fierce. The boy needed a good orthopedic surgeon and surgery to correct a break that hadn't healed properly six months ago, but he wasn't likely to get either. His father was a day laborer, and what money there was went for food and clothes, not health insurance. Surgery, however necessary, was a luxury that was out of reach.

"Don't beat yourself up over this," Mary Littlejohn, his nurse, said quietly from behind him. "You're doing all you can."

"It's not enough," he said flatly, turning away to wash his hands. "That kid's going to live with a limp the rest of his life, and it doesn't have to be that way, dammit. If I could get him to Jeremy Stevens in Jackson—"

Mary cut in with the bluntness of a longtime friend. "But you can't. His parents are proud— they won't take handouts. And you're already helping more people than you can afford to."

"Don't start," he growled.

He might as well have saved his breath. Old enough to be his mother, Mary had been speaking her mind from the first day she came to work for him, three years ago, when he opened the clinic. "Somebody has to say something, and I'm just the person to do it. I know you came home to help people, but you've got to be sensible about it, Greywolf. Half the patients you see never carry through on their promise to pay, and you just let it go. That's no way to run a business. You've got your own bills to pay."

"I'm making it," he said shortly. There was no way he was going to hound people who could barely put groceries on the table for the money for shots for their kids. "Who's next?"

"Jane Birdsong," she said, ticking them off on her fingers. "Then old man Thompson, Bill Parsons, Abigail Wilson, and Rachel Fortune."

Reaching for the Birdsong chart, Luke threw her a sharp glance of surprise. "Fortune? As in one of old lady Kate's brood?"

Mary's faded blue eyes twinkled with amusement. "The one and only. If I remember correctly, this one belongs to Jake...one of the twins, I think."

"And she's here to see *me?*"

Chuckling at his suspicious tone, she nodded. "So she says. Word must have gotten out what a good doctor you are."

He snorted at that. "Get real, Mary. We're talking about the Fortunes, remember? The stinking-rich ones who hang out with the Kennedys and Rockefellers? The old lady had enough money to buy every major hospital in the country—somehow I can't see her granddaughter going to a rural clinic for medical care unless she was dying. Did she look sick?"

"Are you kidding?" she asked. "I'd have given my eye teeth to look that sick at her age. Want me to show her in?"

Curious, Luke nodded. "Room three," he began, only to stop short, scowling. What the hell was he doing? He had sick patients in the waiting room, poor people who would wait without complaint for as long as it took to see him. Rachel Fortune couldn't just waltz in like she owned the place and cut to the head of the line because he couldn't imagine what she wanted with him and her family had more money than God.

"Forget that," he growled. "She can wait her turn just like everyone else. Show Mr. Thompson into three."

"You're the boss," Mary said with a shrug, and went to do his bidding.

When Rocky was shown into an examining room nearly two hours later, she stopped in surprise. "Oh, I'm not here for an exam," she told the nurse hurriedly. "I have a business proposition to discuss with Dr. Greywolf. I know I should have called first, but I was afraid he'd be booked up and it'd be weeks before I could see him."

"And you didn't want to wait," Mary guessed shrewdly, grinning.

Caught in the trap of the older woman's friendly, knowing eyes, Rocky couldn't help but laugh. "What can I say? I was born a month early, and I've been in a hurry ever since. Is it always this busy around here?"

Her blue eyes twinkling, Mary said, "Busy? Today's a slow day. Most nights we're lucky to get out of here by eight." Taking a quick inventory to make sure everything in the room was as it should be, she motioned to the straight-backed chair positioned against the wall. "Have a seat. I hate to tell you this, but you've got another wait. Dr. Greywolf will get to you as soon as possible."

Rocky thanked her, but as soon as the door shut quietly behind the nurse she realized there was no way she was going to be able to just sit there and wait. She was too nervous, too anxious, too excited. For four months now, ever since she'd inherited a helicopter and three single-engine planes from her grandmother, she'd been searching for the perfect locale to start her own flying service. She'd checked out everywhere from Estes Park to Jackson Hole to Vail, and in the end she'd found what she was looking for practically in the backyard of her grandmother's Wyoming ranch.

Shaking her head over her own stupidity, she wondered why she hadn't thought of Clear Springs sooner. It was a small town, rough and rugged and charmingly flavored with the old West, and she'd always loved it. Invitingly situated between the Ghost Mountains to the north and a Shoshone Indian reservation to the south, it drew a respectable number of tourists in the summer and its share of hunters and hikers in the fall and winter. And, incredibly, there were no pilots for hire in the area to take hunters into the mountains or fly search-and-rescue in case of an emergency. The situation couldn't have been better if her grandmother had arranged things for her in heaven.

Which Kate just might have done, she admitted with a rueful flash of dimples. There hadn't been much that Katherine Winfield Fortune hadn't done or tried in life. She'd gone her own way, done her own thing, always with a style that was legendary. She was the one who'd taught Rocky to fly when she was sixteen, and if there was a way to pull strings from heaven, Kate would have found a way.

Memories swamped Rocky. She still found it hard to believe Kate was dead. How could a woman who was so full of spirit, of life, let death take her in a plane crash in some godforsaken jungle? Kate had been tougher than that, stronger. And too good a pilot to let a plane she was flying go down so easily. She would have fought like hell to keep it in the air; and then, when it became clear that wasn't going to be possible, she would have found a way to land the thing. And she would have walked away, dammit. She should have.

Only she hadn't.

Her throat tight, Rocky swallowed. Lord, she missed her. Kate had always understood her need for independence, her need to stand on her own two feet and cut herself free of the Fortune money, Fortune Cosmetics, Fortune *expectations*. And with her death, she'd given her the means to do that. Thanks to Kate, she had her planes, experience flying in the mountains, and the emergency medical training Kate had insisted she take when she got her commercial pilot's license. She'd taken care of everything.

Except a landing field.

Her cousin Kyle, who had inherited her grandmother's ranch, had graciously offered to let her use the facilities there, but Rocky's stubborn pride had refused to let her accept. She'd grown up with advantages most people couldn't even dream of, and it was time she proved she could stand on her own two feet. That meant no favors from family, no free business advice, nothing. She would either succeed or fail, all by herself.

Which meant she still needed an airstrip. And the only other private one in the area was owned by Luke Greywolf.

The place had once belonged to Douglas Aeronautics, and Luke had bought it for a song—not, according to the locals, because he planned to reopen the old flying service that had gone belly-up during the oil embargo of the seventies, but because the land was cheap and close to the reservation. He'd turned the largest building on the property into a clinic and hot-topped the parking lot, but other than that, he'd made few other changes. The hangar was still rusted and the runway pitted and unused, and that was what she wanted to talk to the good doctor about.

She'd heard he was a reasonable man, so she didn't see any reason why they couldn't do business together...except for the clinic sign out front. Made of wood and painted a dull gray, it would have been plain and unobtrusive if not for the face of a wolf that had been carved into the rough wood by a talented hand. She had a sinking feeling that that sign said a lot about Luke Greywolf. If he was anything like the wolf in his name and as protective of his territory, then making a deal with him wasn't going to be quite as easy as she'd hoped.

She wasn't Kate Fortune's granddaughter for nothing, however. Kate had taught her that when a woman wanted something in a man's world, she had to pull out all the stops, and that was just what she'd done. Turning toward the mirror on the wall by the small dressing area, she took a quick inventory of herself and grinned. Lord, she looked like Allie today! Of course, most of the world thought she looked like her twin sister every day, but she knew better. Oh, they were identical right down to their toes, but it was Allie who loved makeup and glamour and had been born with the style that made her the perfect choice as the model for Fortune Cosmetics.

And Rocky didn't envy her one little bit. She would have hated the fuss and bother and never being able to step out in public without worrying about her mascara being smudged or her hair limp. But on a day when she needed everything going for her, Rocky decided with a chuckle, looking like her sister couldn't hurt. Giving her image in the mirror one last critical glance, she nodded, satisfied. If Lucas Greywolf could turn down her proposal when she looked this good, then the man didn't have any blood in his veins.

Luke made a few quick notes in Abigail Wilson's file, his brows knitting as he stared down at comments he'd made after her previous visits. She was pregnant with her sixth child and couldn't afford to feed the five she already had. She seemed cheerful enough, but she couldn't hide the stress in her eyes. Like all the women on the reservation, she wanted more for her children but knew the odds were against them. The lucky ones scraped and fought and found a way out the first chance they got. The rest stayed and struggled just to exist. There was nothing else they could do.

Frustrated, irritated, he closed the file and handed it to Mary. "Rachel Fortune still here?"

She nodded. "Room one. And not one word of complaint out of her when I showed her in there. In fact, she apologized to me for stopping in without an appointment—said she needed to talk to you. I thought she'd be snooty, but she's been real nice."

Reserving judgment, Luke merely grunted. The lady had to want something real bad if she'd sat over two hours in a waiting room full of sick patients to see him when she wasn't even sick. "Yeah, I'm sure she's a regular princess," he drawled, heading for the door. "It shouldn't take long to find out what she wants. Show Christie Eagle and her mother into three and tell them I'll be right with them."

His rugged face set in grim lines, he strode down the hall to examining room one, going over in his head what he knew about the Fortune family. It wasn't much. The old lady, Kate, had died recently in a plane crash, and from what he'd heard about her, she'd been one sharp cookie. She'd ruled the family empire with a firm hand, and if the falling price of Fortune Cosmetics stock was anything to go by, her absence was already being felt.

So what did Kate's granddaughter want with him? he wondered with a frown. They didn't exactly run in the same circles. Apart from her cousin Kyle, whom he occasionally saw in town, he wouldn't know her or the rest of the clan if he passed them on the street. And that was just fine with him. Because of the family's connection to the town, the local paper faithfully reported every tidbit of gossip about the clan, and by all accounts, the younger Fortunes were wild, willful, and spoiled, not to mention attracted to danger. Just last week, he'd read about Rachel's exploits at a charity air show. She'd been performing stunts—stunts, for God's sake!—when her plane nearly stalled. She'd managed to pull out of it, but she could have just as easily crashed and killed not only herself, but dozens of innocent people on the ground.

Luke had little use for that kind of irresponsibility. The whole bunch was too used to doing what they damn well pleased. They flew in to the ranch when they wanted to play cowboy and flew out again when they grew bored with the game. From what he could see, they'd never done a hard day's work in their life.

Reaching the examining room where Rachel waited, he pushed the door open and soundlessly stepped inside to find her standing with her back to him, examining his diploma from medical school, which was framed and hanging on the far wall. Determined to keep this short and sweet, he said, "Ms. Fortune? I understand you wanted to talk to me—"

That was as far as he got. She turned then, a smile of welcome flirting with the edges of her mouth, and he felt the impact clear across the room. Stopping dead in his tracks, he would have sworn she knocked him out of his shoes. *This* was Rachel Fortune?

He'd expected her to be attractive—money and good looks just seemed to go hand in hand—and her grandmother had started one of the most successful cosmetic companies in the world. With good bone structure and skin, not to mention the right makeup, any woman could be reasonably pretty.

Pretty didn't even begin to describe the woman before him, however. With her sculptured cheeks, slanting brows and large dark brown eyes, she could have stopped traffic in any city in the world, but here in Clear Springs, where the harsh winters dried the skin and added years to a woman's face, she was as breathtaking and unexpected as a rose in the snow. And he couldn't stop staring. Tall and slim, she was dressed for business in a somber black wool suit and stark white blouse, but the effect was ruined by the way the fit of the skirt emphasized her slender waist and the impossibly long length of her legs. And then there was her hair. Wine red, it fell in a soft, sweeping curve to her angled jaw, just begging for a man's touch.

He'd always been a sucker for red hair.

The thought slipped up on him like a craving in the night, easing into his blood in a sudden flash of heat that caught him totally off guard. Stunned, he stiffened, guilt and resentment twisting in his gut. He hadn't looked twice at a woman in the two years since Jan had died, and he didn't plan to start now with someone like Lady Fortune here, who had the world at her feet. He only had to see the amusement glinting in those big brown eyes of hers to know that not only was she aware of the effect she had on men, she expected it. If that was what she was here for, she'd made a wasted trip.

"I'm Dr. Greywolf," he said coolly. "What can I do for you, Ms. Fortune?"

Caught in his intense dark brown eyes, Rocky hesitated, her smile wavering and her heart, for no reason that she could understand, suddenly jumping crazily in her breast. Okay, she acknowledged, he was a good-looking man, if you liked the stony type. She didn't. She liked a man who laughed easily, at himself and the world. That did not in any way, shape or form appear to describe Luke Greywolf.

There was no glint of humor in his nearly black eyes, no smile to relieve the lean, chiseled features of his square face. Tall and broad-shouldered in a white lab coat, his straight, inky-black hair cut conservatively short, he stood like a pine in the forest that didn't bend, his proud Shoshone heritage stamped all over him. It was there in the width of his brow, the granite-hard set of his jaw, his blade of a nose. And it was there in his eyes. Never taking his gaze from her, he watched her like a wary hawk that just dared her to make a wrong move.

It wasn't, Rocky decided, swallowing to ease the sudden dryness in her throat, a look she particularly cared for. Her nerve endings bristling, she reminded herself that she didn't have to like the man to do business with him, then gave him a smile that had, in the past, left more than one unsuspecting male panting. "Please . . . call me Rocky."

Far from impressed, he arched a disbelieving brow. "Rocky Fortune? I thought your name was Rachel."

"It is," she said. "But I earned the nickname when I gave my brother a black eye when I was ten, and it just sort of stuck." Crossing the room to him, she held out her hand and grinned. "I've still got a wicked left, but I haven't punched anybody out in years. It's nice to meet you, Doc. I've heard a lot about you."

Most people, upon hearing the story about her nickname, wanted to know what her brother had done to provoke her into punching his lights out, but Luke Greywolf only stared at her hand before reluctantly taking it in a quick shake that was over almost before it had begun. "I understand you wanted to talk to me," he said curtly. "If this is about a contribution to one of the local charities—"

He hadn't so much as moved, but Rocky could feel him mentally pushing her toward the door. "It isn't," she said quickly. "Actually, I have a business proposition for you."

Luke couldn't have been more surprised if she'd said she wanted to buy him a Ferrari. Stepping farther into the room, he shut the door behind him, closing out the noise rolling down the hall from the waiting room. In the sudden silence, his brown eyes, dark with suspicion, met hers. "Is this some kind of joke? You can probably buy and sell me a hundred times over, Ms. Fortune. What kind of business could we possibly have in common?"

"You have an airfield that no one's using," she replied promptly. "I'd like to buy it."

"Why?"

"Because I need it," she said simply. "My grandmother left me a small fleet of planes and a helicopter, and I want to use them to start a flying service here in Clear Springs. You know, fly in hunters and skiers, that kind of thing. There's not anything like that in this area. Everyone goes to Jackson, which is nearly a hundred miles away, not to mention on the other side of the mountains. That's not only inconvenient, it's a loss of revenue for the city. So surely you can see that there's a need . . ."

Luke kept his gaze shuttered. He saw, all right. What he saw was that she needed his landing strip to fly in her rich friends to hunt and party. They'd throw their money around town, look down their noses at everyone, tear up the woods and the roads, then take home trophy elk and deer as if it were their God-given right.

Not if he had anything to say about it, he thought grimly. The muscles in his jaw bunching at the thought, he turned his back on her and opened the door to the hall. "The airfield's not for sale. If that's all you wanted to discuss, I have patients..."

Dismissing her as easily as if she were a door-to-door salesman, he patiently waited for her to precede him into the hall. Caught off guard, Rocky stood right where she was. He was turning her down! she thought in disbelief. No one had ever turned her down without doing her the courtesy of considering her offer, and she found, to her irritation, that she didn't like it. She didn't like it one damn bit!

"Can't we at least talk this out?" she persisted stubbornly. "I could come back at the end of the day."

"What's there to talk about?" His face as hard as the Rockies, he stood at the open doorway, clearly impatient for her to leave. "You want my airstrip to fly your rich friends in for the hunting season so they can all play big white hunter. Sorry, but I'm not interested."

"Big white hunter?" she echoed in confusion. "You make it sound like I'm planning some kind of Jungle Jim party thing."

"Aren't you?"

"No! Oh, sure, I plan to hire out to hunters or anyone else who needs my services, but I have a lot more to offer than tour-guide services. I'm a licensed EMT, Dr. Greywolf," she said proudly. "I've trained with one of the best search-and-rescue teams in the country and logged hundreds of hours flying in the mountains. This community needs that kind of emergency service. And I need an airfield."

"Isn't there one at your grandmother's ranch?"

"That belongs to my cousin Kyle now. I want a place of my own."

"Then you'll have to find one somewhere else. Mine's not for sale."

He was so adamant, Rocky wanted to shake him. It wasn't as if he were using the airstrip, she thought resentfully as the temper she'd inherited along with her red hair from her grandmother started to simmer. It was just sitting there going to pot. It would serve him right if she told him to just forget it. She could buy some land and build what she needed from scratch—but that would take time, dammit, and she wanted to get started now!

"All right," she said abruptly, knowing when she was beating a dead horse. "You don't want to sell. I can respect that. How about leasing it, then? Don't say no," she said quickly, before he could turn her down flat again. "Just think about it for now. The landing strip's just sitting there, not earning you a penny. Maybe you don't need the money personally, but you could always use it to make improvements here at the clinic."

She saw resentment flicker in his eyes and wasn't surprised. He was a proud man, but facts were facts. She'd had more than enough time to look around the place while she waited to talk to him, and it was obvious he was running the place on a shoestring. It was spotlessly clean, but the old building really needed some cosmetic work, work that could easily be paid for with the generous lease she was willing to pay.

Grabbing a piece of paper from her purse, she hurriedly jotted down her telephone number and address, then pushed it into his hand. "If you change your mind, just give me a call."

She didn't give him time to tell her hell would freeze over before he made that call. Stepping around him, her bearing as regal as a queen's, she walked down the hall and turned the corner into the reception area. Staring after her, Luke crushed the slip of paper with her phone number in his fist and swore. "Brat," he muttered, tossing the note into a nearby trash can. "Who the hell does she think she is? She's got all the money in the world, and all she can think about is her damn airfield. If she thinks she's got problems, let her talk to Michael Hawk. Or Abigail Wilson. *They're* the ones who could use her money—"

"Which is why you should have at least considered what she had to say," Mary retorted from the supply closet, which was conveniently located right next to examining room one. Making no apologies for the fact that she had blatantly eavesdropped, not only on his conversation with himself but also on his meeting with Rocky Fortune, she frowned at him disapprovingly. "It's not like you're using that airstrip. And the money you'd make on a lease would go a long way toward financing Michael Hawk's operation."

"His father won't accept help, remember?"

"A handout, no. But Rocky was right—this place could use some work. You could hire Mr. Hawk to do it. That would save his pride, and Michael would still get his surgery."

She had a point, Luke grudgingly admitted, one he hadn't even considered. Damn! What the hell was wrong with him? He should have thought of Michael himself, but he'd been so busy drooling over the lady he couldn't think straight. And then there was the money. She had it in spades, so she was used to getting what she wanted because she wanted it. And that had rubbed him the wrong way. So he'd cut off his nose to spite his face, just to bring her down a peg or two. Idiot!

"I'll talk to her," he said stiffly. "Later."

"And you'll apologize?"

He rolled his eyes, his lips twitching. Trust Mary to insist on a pound of flesh. "All right, I'll apologize for being rude and obnoxious. Now can we get back to work? In case you've forgotten, we still got patients to see."

"In a minute," she said, and stepped into the first waiting room to retrieve the crumpled slip of paper he'd tossed in the trash. When she placed it in his hand and closed his fingers around it, she was grinning. "You can't call her if you haven't got her number." Chuckling, she turned away to retrieve Christie Eagle's chart.

The small fifty-year-old wood-frame house was showing serious signs of age. Even in the dark shadows of the night, Luke could see the peeling paint, the slightly uneven steps of the porch, the shutters that probably hadn't hung straight in decades. Surprised, he braked to a stop at the curb and grabbed the wrinkled scrap of paper he'd tossed on the dash when he left the clinic a few minutes earlier. A quick glance at the address Rocky had scrawled there four hours earlier assured him he'd made no mistake. This was it—the place where Kate Fortune's granddaughter was living.

It made no sense, he told himself as he approached the front steps. He didn't know anything about the details of the old lady's will, apart from what Rocky had told him, but it was a given that she wasn't strapped for funds. She could, no doubt, afford the best that Clear Springs had to offer. So what was she doing living here?

Bothered more than he should have been by the question, he knocked briskly on the door, determined not to get caught up in the intriguing diversity that was Rocky Fortune. The lady had her quirks and the money to indulge them. He didn't care what she did as long as she agreed to pay him a decent lease on the airfield.

Knocking again, he frowned when there was no answer. Someone was obviously home—he could see the lights through the covered windows, and the walls were practically vibrating from the country-and-western song being belted out on a radio inside. "What the hell?" he muttered, and tried the knob. It opened without a sound. Surprised, he scowled. Crazy girl, didn't she know better than to leave her door unlocked at night? Clear Springs might not be much of a metropolis, but just like anywhere else, it had its fair share of crime.

Giving the door a slight nudge, he stepped cautiously inside and found himself in a small entrance hall. On the radio, a whiskey-voiced man was singing about a honky-tonk woman, but Luke hardly noticed. Through the arched doors that led to the living room he caught sight of Rocky, and he could do nothing but stare. This was, he knew, the same woman who'd come sashaying into his clinic earlier that afternoon, dressed to kill and flashing her money around. The expensive business suit, however, had been traded for paint-spattered jeans and a ragtag cotton shirt, her high heels for a pair of tennis shoes that looked as if they'd been through a war. Standing with her back to him, her wild red hair covered with a blue bandanna, she was painting the living room and singing her heart out, while her slim hips kept heart-stopping time to the beat of the music. Feeling like he'd been struck by lightning on a clear day, Luke stood as if turned to stone, while deep inside a hot pulse kept time with every sway of her hips.

Belting out the current number one country hit, Rocky turned to add paint to her dry roller pan— and nearly dropped it, stunned when she saw Luke Greywolf standing in the doorway. She should have laughed—she was a mess, with white paint in her

hair and on her clothes and even under her fingernails, and her singing had often been compared to
a cat's screeching. But there was something in his
eyes that wasn't the least bit funny, and suddenly
her chest seemed tight and breathing wasn't nearly
as easy as it had been before she spied him in the
doorway.

Flustered, she hit the power switch to the radio.
"Well, this is a surprise," she said, too loudly,
shattering the sudden silence. "I wasn't expecting
to see you this evening."

"I knocked," he said stiffly. "But the radio—"

"Was blaring," she finished for him, grinning.
"I have to crank it up to max when I sing, or I'd
have every dog in the neighborhood howling at the
moon."

For a moment, she thought she saw a smile start
to curl up the corners of his mouth, and she found
herself waiting expectantly, her gaze fastened on his
lips. But then his eyes fell to the roller and pan at
her feet, the paint on her arms and clothes, and a
confused anger hardened his face. Scowling at her,
he growled, "Tell me something, lady. Just what
the hell kind of game are you playing, anyway?"

Taken aback by the unexpected attack, Rocky
blinked. "Game? What are you talking about?"

"This handyman routine," he retorted, waving
at the drop sheets and painting paraphernalia that

littered the living room. "I didn't think you people cut up your own meat, let alone knew how to yield a paintbrush."

Outraged, Rocky gasped, her brown eyes narrowing dangerously. *"Cut up our own meat?"*

It was the wrong thing to say. Luke knew it the second the words left his mouth, and he wanted to kick himself. What was it about this woman that knocked him off kilter so easily? He'd never had a problem communicating with women before—he liked them, dammit! But there was something about Rocky Fortune that just seemed to rub him the wrong way.

Heat climbing up his throat, he quickly backpedaled. "I didn't mean that the way it sounded. It's just that your family is rolling in dough, and you're probably not used to doing things for yourself—"

"Like tying my own shoelaces?"

Luke winced at the sweetly purred gibe. "You're not going to make this easy for me, are you?"

"Not on your life," she retorted, beginning to enjoy herself. "So what can I do for you, Doc? You didn't show up here just to insult me."

She knew, dammit, why he was there—he could see the anticipation dancing in her eyes. And she was going to make him squirm. Amused in spite of himself, he swallowed his pride and admitted, "I've given it some thought and realized I may have rejected your offer to lease the airstrip too quickly. I thought maybe we could discuss terms.''

''Terms, huh?'' she echoed, grinning. ''I think I can manage that.'' Whisking off the sheets covering the furniture, she motioned to him to take a seat in an overstuffed chair, then settled opposite him on a faded brocade coach. ''Okay, Doc, the ball's in your court. It's your serve. Give it your best shot.''

He named a sum that he thought was more than fair, only to have her gasp as if he'd just insulted her. ''You've got to be kidding! That's highway robbery. Have you looked at the runway recently? And the hangar?''

She threw out a figure that was half the one he'd named, he countered, and the game began. With a skill Luke couldn't help but admire, she held her ground and bartered like a horse trader, making no attempt to hide the fact that she was in her element. Later, it would bother him that he'd enjoyed himself so much, but when he rose to leave nearly an hour after he arrived, they had a deal.

Confident that he'd gotten the best of her, he solemnly shook hands with her, then couldn't resist gigging her as she walked him to the door. ''You drive a hard bargain, lady. But I would have taken less, you know.''

Unperturbed, she only grinned. "Really? That's good to know, Doc. Because I would have paid more." Her brown eyes sparkling, she laughed and shut the door in his face.

Two

The snow that had been falling all day had finally stopped, but the night was dark as pitch and cold as the devil. Flipping off the clinic lights, Lucas stepped outside and locked the front door, swearing under his breath as the wind seemed to cut right through his clothes. With a sharp jerk, he tugged the zipper of his down jacket as high as it would go, but it didn't help. Nothing did when the temperature was dropping like a rock toward zero and a twenty-mile-an-hour wind was blowing fit to kill. Leaning into the gale, his shoulders hunched against the cold that snaked down the back of his neck, he hurried toward his Bronco at the far end of the clinic's small parking lot and quickly climbed inside.

It wasn't until he stuck the key in the ignition and started the motor and the heater, though, that he allowed himself to even glance toward the hangar that he'd leased to Rocky Fortune a week ago. A hulking shadow in the night on the far side of the runway, it was bathed in light, just as it had been every night that week. And for some gnawing reason that he couldn't have explained, that irritated the hell out of him.

When he agreed to lease the place to her, he'd told himself the lady wasn't going to be a problem. Because of the security deposit and first and last months' rent she'd paid him, Michael Hawk had gotten his operation, and that was all he cared about. If that black pickup of hers was parked in front of the hangar when he got to work in the morning and was still there when he left at night, drawing his eye every time he stepped outside, he'd just learn to ignore it and her.

Yeah, yeah, he thought bitterly. Even on a bad-hair day, Rocky Fortune wasn't the type of woman a man could easily ignore. And it was damn frustrating! What the hell was she doing in there, anyway? Didn't she ever go home? And why did he care?

He didn't, he told himself flatly. Not a lick. She had a lease—the place was hers to do with as she liked. She could move a cot in and sleep there for all he cared, as long as she left him alone. If he was curious, it was just because he couldn't imagine what she was doing in there. When they struck their deal, he'd warned her the hangar had to be renovated before she could use it, but he had yet to see a work crew there. And he didn't believe for a sec-

ond that she was making the necessary improvements herself. Not a Fortune. She might have
slapped a couple of coats of paint on the walls of
that old house she was renting, but when it came to
work, the hard, physical, dirty kind that got under
your nails and stained your clothes and skin and
left you bone-weary at the end of the day, she'd
probably never done a smidgen of it in her spoiled
little life.

His hands curling around the steering wheel, he
glared at the hanger's blazing lights and told himself that whatever Rocky was doing, it was none of
his business. But when he put the Bronco in gear,
he headed for the hangar instead of home, cursing
himself all the way.

With a low moan, the wind whistled around the
hangar, searching and finding a way in through the
cracks and crevices of the old sliding metal door. In
the corner, the heater was working overtime blowing, but it did little good against the chilly air that
crept around her ankles. Shivering, Rocky tried to
ignore it as she bent over the metal worktable she
was sanding so that she could paint it in the morning, but her toes and fingers were nearly numb from
the cold. She was, she decided, going to have to call
it a night soon. Then, tomorrow, she was going to
do something about that door. And get another

heater—she could see right now that one just wasn't
going to be enough. The plumbing in the bathroom needed to be checked over, and then she'd
have to see about getting someone out there to haul
away all the rusty junk that had been left behind by
the previous occupant. It had taken her most of the
week to go through it all, salvaging what she could,
then piling the discarded pieces neatly in a corner.
But it couldn't stay there—

Without warning, the outer door adjacent to the
hangar's small office suddenly flew open, sending
a blast of icy wind rushing inside. Startled, her
heart jumping into her throat, Rocky glanced up
just in time to see Lucas Greywolf blow in with the
wind.

Over the course of the past week, she'd spent
every waking hour at the hangar and she hadn't
caught sight of the doc once, which was just fine
with her. He'd made no secret of the fact that he
didn't approve of her, and that still galled her. Not
that she cared what he thought of her, she was
quick to assure herself. She had her own agenda
and wasn't looking for a man. Especially one who
was so quick to look down that proud nose of his
and find her lacking. That didn't mean, however,
that she'd forgotten how just the sight of him had
made her stomach flutter.

Had he noticed? she wondered, and winced at the thought. She'd been expecting a middle-aged, paunchy doctor in a white lab coat, not a tall, lean hunk who could have just stepped out of one those sexy cigarette ads. If she'd been momentarily thrown for a loop, it was a natural enough reaction. He'd just caught her by surprise—that was all. The next time she ran into him, she'd promised herself, she wouldn't bat an eye.

Well, here it is—the next time—Rocky, my girl, a voice drawled in her ear, *and not only are you not batting an eye, you're not breathing, either. Try not to drool, sweetie. It's so tacky. And the good doctor just might get the mistaken impression that you're interested. You're not, are you?*

Her heart stumbled. Of course she wasn't! The last man she'd made the mistake of getting interested in had left a bruise on her heart that was only just now starting to heal. Greg Butler. Just the thought of him brought a bad taste to her mouth and put her off even looking at another man. If Lucas Greywolf caught her attention, it was only because she couldn't figure him out. Every time she saw him, he was scowling, and tonight was no different. Did he never smile? Openly studying him, she watched him sweep his cowboy hat off and knock the snow from it and assured herself she wasn't even close to drooling. Just because she wasn't buying, however, didn't mean she couldn't window shop.

"Hey, Doc." She greeted him easily as she reluctantly returned her attention to the rusty table she was sanding with a wire brush. "You picked a heck of a night to come calling. Sorry I can't give you the guided tour, but I've sort of got my hands in this right now, and I want to finish before I close up shop for the night."

If he hadn't seen it with his own two eyes, Lucas would have never believed it. The oh-so-rich, born-with-a-gold-not-silver-spoon-in-her-mouth Ms. Fortune was actually working. Her face free of makeup, her worn jeans and faded college sweatshirt splattered with dirt and grime, she scrubbed at the metal table she was refinishing with a total disregard for the rust she was getting all over her. Her hands were stained with the stuff, splotches of it had settled on her cheeks and neck, and she even had it under her fingernails. Yet she still somehow managed to look beautiful. How the hell did she do it?

Disgusted with himself for even noticing, Lucas dragged his eyes away from her and glanced around in surprise. If the lady had done this all by herself in just a week, she'd really been hustling. She'd cleaned the place up, collected all the old motor parts in a pile in the corner, then scrubbed decades of grease from large patches of the cement floor. There was still a lot of work left to be done, but she'd made more of a dent than he'd expected, and he had to admit he was impressed. He hadn't thought the lady had it in her.

As if reading his thoughts, she laughed softly. "Don't look now, Doc, but your chin's on the floor. What's the matter? Did you think the spoiled little rich girl was too finicky to get her hands dirty?"

The teasing gibe struck home. Heat, brick red and uncomfortable, rose in a tide from his neck to his cheeks, making it impossible for him to deny the accusation. So he did the only thing a man with any integrity could—he looked her right in the eye and baldly told her exactly what he thought of her. "To be perfectly honest, I didn't think you'd even know where to begin. But then again, spoiled little rich girls aren't exactly my field of expertise."

"So what is?"

He frowned. "What?"

"Your field of expertise," she answered patiently, knowing she shouldn't push the issue, but unable to drop it. Just what type of woman attracted a man like Lucas Greywolf? And why was that information suddenly so important to her? "And I'm not talking about medicine, Doc. You're what—thirty? Thirty-two?"

"Thirty-five."

"And well preserved for your advanced age," she said teasingly. "Men like you, especially when they've got *M.D.* behind their names, don't usually walk around loose. You must have to sweep the women off your front porch every night just to get inside your house."

Something flickered in his eyes, something she couldn't quite read before it was quickly shuttered behind a glint of amusement. "Yeah, life's rough. So what do you want to know? How short or tall I like my women, and if you fit the mold?"

"No! Or course not!"

Flustered, she glanced away and inadvertently jerked her hand across a rough, jagged corner of the table she was sanding. The rusty edge, as sharp as a razor, cut right across the pad of her thumb, slicing it open. "Damn!"

"What's wrong?"

Her teeth clenched tight to hold in the curses that rose to her tongue, Rocky pressed the wound against her middle, cradling the injured hand close. "Nothing," she said tersely. "Just a scrape."

"The hell it is. You're white as a sheet." Crossing the hanger in four swift strides, he reached for her hand. "Let me see, Rocky," he said quietly. "In case you haven't noticed, you're bleeding all over that dirty shirt of yours."

She wanted to deny it, but anything that hurt this bad had to be bleeding like a stuck pig. Reluctantly letting him take her hand, she winced as he gently turned it over to expose the two-inch cut at the base of her thumb. Blood seeped from it, flooding her palm.

His expression grim, Lucas looked up from the wound to her ashen face. "You're not going to pass out on me now, are you?"

She gave him a withering look that her grandmother would have been proud of. "A Fortune woman faint at the sight of a little blood? Kate would turn over in her grave. How bad is it?"

He probed gently, not wanting to hurt her, but knowing there was no avoiding it. "It's in an awkward spot," he finally announced, glancing back up at her with a frown. "Every time you move your thumb it's going to break open if you don't have it stitched. How long has it been since you've had a tetanus shot?"

Caught off guard, she blinked. "I don't know. Maybe a couple of years. I can't remember."

"Then it's probably been longer than you think. You'll need another one." Pulling a clean, neatly folded handkerchief from the back pocket of his jeans, he wrapped it around her hand and stanched the flow of blood as best he could. Glancing around for her jacket, he found a forest-green down coat hanging on a hook near the door and helped her into it. "Come on, let's go." Hustling her out the door and into his Bronco, he quickly drove her over to the clinic.

Rocky protested that all the fuss wasn't necessary—if he'd just give her the tetanus shot, she'd clean the wound herself and slap a butterfly bandage on it when she got home—but Lucas wasn't listening. Ushering her into one of the examining rooms, he took her coat from her, settled her in a chair and collected the supplies he needed. All business, he took time only to wash his hands and make sure she wasn't allergic to any medications before he pulled up a stool next to her and reached for her injured hand.

Over the course of the years, he'd lost track of the number of cuts and gashes he'd cleaned and stitched, and he could normally do it with his eyes closed. But his knees brushed hers, his concentration wavered, and suddenly nothing was as it should be. Her scent, subtle and spicy and damned provocative, reached out to him, teasing his senses, distracting him. Why hadn't he noticed in the hangar how soft her skin was? How delicate her fingers were? With no trouble whatsoever, he could imagine those same fingers touching him, caressing him—

"Doc?"

Her husky query seemed to reach right inside him and pull him out of the fantasy that had come out of nowhere to swamp him in heat. Jerking his eyes up to hers, he found her watching him with an amused, puzzled frown. Swallowing a curse, he stiffened. "Yeah?"

"You're looking at my hand like you've never seen one before. Is everything okay?"

Hell, no, it wasn't okay, he almost snapped. How could it be when she was hurt and bleeding and all he could think of was how good she smelled? What the devil had she done to him? "Everything's fine," he growled. "Just peachy. Give me a second to clean this up, and you can get out of here." And out of his life, he silently promised himself. Because just as soon as he had the lady patched up, he swore he wasn't going anywhere near her again. Not if just touching her did this to him.

His face carved in harsh lines, he went to work and had the wound cleaned and stitched in no time. Her gaze carefully directed away from his handiwork, she stared at the far wall and chatted about the progress she was making at the hangar, the mechanic she had hired, who would start tomorrow, the coming of Christmas and the shopping she still had to do. He put seven stitches at the base of her thumb, bandaged the cut and gave her a tetanus shot after she rolled up her sleeve, and she didn't so much as whimper.

What did you expect? a voice drawled in his head. *She's Fortune-tough, just like her grandmother.*

Then she turned toward him, and he felt as if someone had punched him hard in the gut when he saw for the first time the tears welling in her eyes. "Are you all right?"

She nodded, a crooked smile pushing up one corner of her mouth as she hastily swiped at her still-pale cheeks. "Don't pay any attention to me," she said thickly, laughing shakily. "I'm fine. Really."

"Then why are you crying? Did I hurt you?"

"No! Oh, no," she quickly assured him. "I'm just a lousy patient. I didn't feel anything once you deadened it, but I could just imagine this needle going in and out—"

Turning slightly green, she swallowed and quickly abandoned that line of thought. Straightening her shoulders with a visible effort, she warned teasingly, "You realize, of course, that if you tell anybody I was bawling like a baby over a few stitches, I'll be forced to deny it."

Fighting a smile, he nodded, his expression deliberately solemn. "My lips are sealed."

It was the wrong thing to say. Her gaze immediately flew to his mouth, and suddenly the air between them was sparking with the kind of hushed expectancy that invariably proceeded an approaching storm. Giving in to impulse, to insanity, he reached for her and captured that beautiful face of hers in his hands, bringing her mouth to his.

The instant his lips settled over hers, he knew it had been too long since he'd kissed a woman, too long since he'd allowed himself to even think about needing one. He was in no shape to handle one like Rocky Fortune. Surprise held her motionless under his hands, but then her mouth softened under his and she was like heat lightning in a bottle... wild, hot, unpredictable. Too late, he realized that she had what it took to make a man sweat in the darkest, coldest part of the night.

The thought lodged in the back of his brain, throbbing like a railroad warning light, but he couldn't focus on anything but the taste of her, the feel of her, the *heat* of her. God, he couldn't even remember the last time he'd felt any kind of female warmth. He just wanted to hold her and kiss her and not think about anything except how good it felt. With a groan that came from the depths of his soul, he slanted his mouth across hers and took the kiss deeper.

Dazed, boneless, clinging to him, Rocky tried to remember Greg and how he had hurt her, but the only image that came to mind was Lucas with his dark, wary eyes and rugged face. He kissed her with a desperation that stole her breath and set her pulse thrumming with a blind, lonely need that was as plaintive and heart-tugging as the call of a wolf on a cold winter night. Her head spinning, she frantically ordered herself to stop this madness right now, but in the dark, wet, hidden recesses of her mouth, his tongue wooed and cajoled and sweetly seduced. Shuddering, her hands climbing up his arms, she moaned and crowded closer, lost to everything but the pleasure drizzling through her like warm honey.

The second her injured hand molded itself to his shoulder, however, pain flared in her palm like a struck match, so hot she could practically smell the sulfur. Her cry muffled against his mouth, she jerked back, breathing hard, and stared at him in dismay. Dear God, what was she doing? This was Lucas Greywolf, her landlord, for heaven's sake, the man who thought she was spoiled and pampered and walked around with her nose in the air and hundred-dollar bills hanging out of her pockets. He was arrogant and condescending and judgmental, and she'd *kissed* him! She had to be losing her mind.

Heat stealing into her cheeks, determined not to let him see how he had shaken her, she let out her breath in a huff and forced a cheeky grin. "Well. If that was an attempt to kiss it and make it better, you were more than a little off the mark, Doc."

He was not amused. His jaw was as rigid as granite. "What it was was inexcusable. I wouldn't blame you if you slapped my face."

"C'mon, Doc, it was just a kiss." She laughed with pretended nonchalance. "Don't sweat it. And thanks for the stitch job. Don't forget to send me a bill." Grabbing her coat, she headed for the door, trying not to run.

Ten seconds later, the front door slammed, leaving behind a silence that was as cold and deep as the snow piling up outside. Standing flat-footed in the examining room where she'd left him, feeling as if he'd been run over by a truck, Lucas stared after her and started to swear.

Bustling into Lucas's private office three days later, Mary caught him scowling out the window at the hangar in the distance and hurriedly bit back a smile. Lucas wasn't normally a brooder, but he'd spent most of the day staring out the window—at the hangar—whenever there was a lull in patients. And she had a feeling his interest in the old place had nothing to do with planes.

Her eyes starting to dance with expectation, she laid the day's mail on his desk, then said casually, "I've been going over the invitation list for the Christmas party, and it seems to be missing a few names."

He turned, his scowl still in place. "Oh, yeah? Who?"

"Judge Ryan," she replied promptly. "Since he bought the old Carson place, he's practically a neighbor."

"You're right," he agreed. "I should have thought of him myself. Go ahead and put him on the list."

"What about Rocky Fortune?"

The look he shot her would have done one of his fierce Shoshone ancestors proud. Mary didn't even blink. "What about her?"

"What about her?" Mary echoed, amused by his deliberate obtuseness. "Lucas, you're leasing the hangar to her! Don't you think it would be rude not to invite her to the only party you give all year?"

"Not at all," he said curtly, his gut clenching just at the thought of seeing her again. He'd spent most of the night fighting off the memory of a kiss that never should have happened, and his obsession with her hadn't improved with the light of day. Damn the woman, he could still taste her, still feel her against him—

Swearing under his breath, he picked up the mail Mary had brought in and blindly flipped through it. "It's not like she's a friend or anything. We have a business arrangement, nothing more."

"But—"

"And she probably wouldn't come, anyway. We don't exactly run in the same circles, you know."

"Then it won't hurt to send her an invitation," Mary said promptly, grinning. "Just as a courtesy."

Tossing down the mail, he growled, "Don't waste a stamp."

Mary shrugged, as if to say that was fine with her, but there was a glint of mischief in her eye that Lucas would have immediately recognized if he had seen it. He didn't. Deliberately turning toward the door, she quickly brought the subject back to work. "Elizabeth Crow's here. She thinks she wrenched her back carrying in firewood. I'll show her into room two."

When she got the invitation in the mail, Rocky stared at it long and hard. There had to be a mistake. The doc might have kissed her until her toes curled, but she wasn't fooling herself into thinking that he liked her. In fact, she seemed to have a talent for getting under his skin. He'd gone out of his way to avoid her ever since he'd kissed her. So why had he invited her to his Christmas party?

"What's that?"

Glancing up from her confused thoughts, Rocky smiled at Charlie Short, her new mechanic. He'd been the first one to answer the ad she placed in the local paper, and she'd only had to talk to him five minutes to know that he was just the man she was looking for. As short as his name, wiry and pushing sixty, he was gruff and blunt and not shy about giving her advice when he thought she needed it. And what he didn't know about planes wasn't worth mentioning. Over the past two days, he'd gone over the fleet she'd inherited from her grandmother, and he had every engine purring like a kitten.

"Nothing," she said with a shrug. "Just an invitation to Dr. Greywolf's Christmas party next week."

"Hey, great! I've heard about those parties of his—the food's supposed to be something else. You're going, aren't you?"

Her heart took a dive just at the thought of getting anywhere near the man anytime soon. She didn't want to see him, didn't want to socialize with him, didn't want to look into his eyes and think about a kiss that had haunted her sleep for the past five nights.

"It's just one of those courtesy things," she said stiffly, tossing the invitation in the trash. "I don't think there's much point in going."

"Are you kidding?" Snatching up the invitation, he looked at her as if she'd lost her mind. "Dammit, girl, where's your head? Just about anyone who's anyone in Clear Springs is going to be at that shindig. And you should be, too! You need to get out and mingle with the locals and let them know that you're open and ready for business. This is a chance for some free advertising, for God's sake! Take advantage of it."

He had a point, one that Rocky would have given just about anything to deny. But she wasn't Kate Fortune's granddaughter for nothing. As much as she wanted to avoid Lucas like a bad case of the measles, she couldn't let her own personal likes and dislikes interfere with sound business decisions.

"Oh, all right, all right," she muttered. "I'll go. If we can pick up some business, I guess it'll be worth all the fuss."

She didn't plan to stay long, only as long as it took to put in an appearance, scout out the guests for hunters and guides who could possibly use her services and pass around her business card to anyone who happened to express an interest. But the second she stepped through the clinic's front door,

she knew she wasn't going to get out of there anytime soon. The place was wall-to-wall people.
Laughing and talking and nibbling on food that
smelled absolutely fabulous, they were packed in
shoulder to shoulder and could hardly move. And
nobody seemed to care.

Mary Littlejohn, spying her hovering near the
doorway, plowed her way through the bodies and
greeted her like a long-lost daughter. "Rocky! I'm
so glad you came! C'mon, there's someone I want
you to meet."

Not giving her time to do anything but sputter a
greeting, Luke's nurse hauled her through the
crowd and stopped in front of a middle-aged man
who was already deeply involved in a conversation
with a woman Rocky recognized as the mayor.
"Sorry to interrupt," she said in an easy tone that
was anything but regretful, "but I want you two to
meet Rocky Fortune. Rocky, this is Mayor
Whacker and Thomas Gustafson. I was telling
them earlier about your new flying service, and they
were very interested in it."

"You're one of Jake's daughters," Thomas said,
pleased, as he shook her hand. "I can't tell you how
delighted I was when Mary told us you'd moved to
Clear Springs to set up your business. I own the
Black Bear Motel and get requests all the time from
guests who just want to hire a small plane to fly

them into the mountains for some trophy big-horns, and I have to send them to Jackson. This is great! Just great."

Smiling, Mayor Louise Whacker agreed. "We've needed the services you're providing for a long time, dear. Especially search-and-rescue. Your grandmother would be so proud of you."

That started a conversation about Kate, and then the mayor spotted one of the town bigwigs that she insisted Rocky meet. Before Rocky quite realized it, she'd been there well over an hour and enjoyed every second of it. Then she spied Lucas towering head and shoulders over most of the crowd.

She'd known she'd have to speak to him, of course—she couldn't just show up at his party and ignore the man—but she planned to keep it short and sweet, then get the heck out of there. What she didn't plan was for her heart to stop in midbeat at the sight of him.

Damn the man, he had no right to look so good, she thought, shaken. Casually dressed in a white shirt and a red V-necked sweater that did incredible things for his broad shoulders, he was talking to a small, wizened man and laughing at something he had to bend his head to catch. Transfixed, Rocky could do nothing but stare. It was a sight that she knew would follow her into her dreams.

* * *

Still chuckling over Whitey Walker's latest joke, Lucas felt the touch of eyes on him and glanced up, only to suck in a sharp breath at the sight of Rocky staring at him from across the room. He didn't have to ask what she was doing there—Mary's innocent smile when he found her in the crowd had told him all he needed to know. She'd invited her, in spite of his direct order not to.

"Pretty girl," Whitey drawled, noting his sudden distraction. "That's Kate's granddaughter, isn't it?"

Lucas nodded. "Yeah. One of Jake's girls—Rachel."

"The one they call Rocky," the old man said knowingly. "She's got the look of her grandmother. And all her spunk, from what I hear. Word is, she gave old Jake more than a few of those gray hairs of his. A regular daredevil she is. And she's eyeing you like you're the next best thing to sliced bread." Grinning up at Lucas, his black eyes danced with mischief. "So what are you standing here humoring an old man for? Go talk to her, son."

He didn't want to go anywhere near her, but she was his guest, whether he wanted her to be or not, and his mama hadn't raised him to be rude, especially not to a woman. "I'll be right back," he said. "Don't run off."

He'd be polite, make sure **she** was enjoying herself, then find an excuse to put some space between them for the rest of the evening, he promised himself as he started toward her. Considering the number of people he still had to speak to, that wouldn't be hard to do.

Catching up with her, however, proved to be more difficult than he'd expected. He'd hardly taken three steps before one of his mothers-to-be latched on to him and worriedly confided that she thought she might be going into labor three months early. By the time he'd questioned her and determined that she was just being the tiniest bit paranoid, Rocky was nowhere in sight.

Scowling, he went looking for her, got waylaid by one of his elderly patients, then stopped by the police chief for a lengthy conversation about the pros and cons of lowering the speed zone in front of his clinic because of the amount of traffic that was always coming in and out of there. Impatient, he broke away as soon as he could manage with the excuse that he needed to check to see how the food was holding out. Finally, breaking through a group blocking the entrance to the waiting area, he caught up with Rocky near the front door, just as she pulled her coat from the coat rack.

Walking up behind, he took it from her before she even knew he was there. "Sneaking out, Ms. Fortune?" he taunted softly. "And without even a proper thank-you to your host. Tsk, tsk. What would your grandmother say?"

Startled, Rocky whirled with a gasp, her hand flying to the pulse that was suddenly thundering irritatingly at the base of her throat. What was it about this man that had her always off balance? He hadn't even touched her, and her knees were already weak. It was downright embarrassing.

"I wasn't sneaking," she lied. "You were busy and I didn't want to bother you. I was going to send you a note tomorrow telling you how much I enjoyed myself, but now I won't have to do that." Using the manners she'd been taught as a child, she said sweetly, "It was a wonderful party, Dr. Greywolf. Thank you for inviting me. Good night."

She started to reach for her coat, but before she could take it from him, Mary appeared at the door to the waiting room, her smile wide and devilment dancing in her eyes. "Oh, good, I see you found it."

Confused, Rocky looked around. "Found what? My coat? It wasn't lost."

"No, the mistletoe." Mary laughed, nodding to a spot above their heads. "Go ahead, Lucas. Kiss her."

Three

Mortified color staining her cheeks, Rocky should have said something flirty, then gotten the heck out of there. But her brain shut down and her heart started to pound and all she could think of was that first sizzling kiss he'd given her days ago. As flustered as a virgin, she instinctively took a step backward. "Oh, no! That's not necessary—"

His dark eyes starting to twinkle, Lucas arched a brow at her. "What's this? The fearless Rocky Fortune, unnerved by a tiny sprig of mistletoe?" he teased. "It's just a little kiss between friends."

She wanted to protest that they weren't friends—how could they be when they seemed to continually rub each other the wrong way?—and she had a feeling there was no such thing as a *little* kiss where he was concerned. But before she could get the words out, he leaned down and brushed a kiss on her flushed cheek. She felt the fleeting warmth of his lips, a whisper of breath against her skin, and then he was stepping back, his grin crooked as he gauged her reaction.

"There. See? No harm done," he assured her lightly as he held her coat out for her to slip into. "Where'd you park? I'll walk you to your pickup."

Her heartbeat still drumming in her ears, Rocky automatically turned her back on him and eased her arms into the sleeves. "I had to park in the street, but it's not that far. Anyway, you don't need to walk me out. You have guests."

"Who won't miss me for the few minutes it takes to see you to your truck," he said firmly. Grabbing his own coat, he quickly tugged it on.

"He's right, dear," Mary said, adding her two cents. "You're not used to Wyoming winters. It doesn't take long for ice to build up. If you slipped and fell in the dark, it could be a while before anyone found you."

Rocky could have pointed out that she'd dealt with ice and harsh winters in Minneapolis for years, but Lucas already had the door open and was waiting patiently for her to precede him. From the challenging glint in his eye, it was obvious that he was prepared to wait as long as necessary. "Oh, all right," she said with a sigh. "But if you walk all your guests to their cars, you're going to have frostbite before the night's over."

"I'm a doctor," he reminded her, chuckling. "I know how to treat it. Let's go."

The second they stepped outside and shut the door behind them, they might have been the only two people in the world. Silence engulfed them, broken only by the low, mournful moan of the wind as it whipped around them like a living thing, circling them, touching them with icy fingers as they hurried across the crowded parking lot.

Her shoulders hunched against the cold, Rocky kept her eyes focused on the snow-covered ground, all her senses attuned to the man who fell into step beside her. He didn't say a word, but the crunch of his boots was loud in the crystal clear silence, the puff of his breath mingling with hers on the crisp night air. If she hadn't known better, she would have sworn she could even hear the steady thump of his heart beating in time with hers.

The cold's numbed your brain, girl, the voice of reason said tartly in her ear. *The only thing you can hear is your own imagination working overtime. The doc didn't follow you out here into this icebox because he wanted a stroll in the moonlight—he just didn't want you falling on his property and suing the bejeebers out of him. So don't start getting all breathless over nothing. He's just covering himself.*

The thought stung, and it shouldn't have. Wasn't she just here to drum up business? Not willing to delve into that too deeply, she sighed in relief when they finally reached her pickup, which was at the end of a long line of cars that were parked on either side of the road in front of the clinic. "Okay, you've done your duty," she said with a smile as she turned to face him, "and without a single mishap. See, I told you this wasn't necessary."

Standing in the dark, far from the parking-lot lights, Lucas silently acknowledged that she was right. Escorting her to her truck hadn't been all that necessary. But suddenly kissing her was.

He didn't know where the need came from, but suddenly it was a hot, hard fist in his gut, one that wouldn't be put off with a wimpy brush of his lips against her cheek. He wanted a full-fledged, breath-stealing, knee-buckling kiss, the kind that a man could lose sleep over just thinking about. And he wanted it now, from Rocky Fortune.

You're out of your mind, Greywolf. A few sandwiches short of a picnic. Just how many glasses of Mary's rum punch did you have?

Staring down at her in the darkness, he told himself not to do something stupid that he was going to regret later. All he had to do was wish her good-night, then turn around and walk away, while he still could. It was that simple.

But almost from the beginning nothing had been simple with this woman. And tonight was no different. She got under a man's skin like a rash and just didn't go away, dammit! He'd tried to ignore her, to keep his distance, to distract himself with his other guests, but nothing had worked. Muttering curses under his breath, he knew there was no way in hell he was going to walk away.

Reaching for her, he saw her eyes widen, and he murmured, "I know you're probably going to belt me for this, but there doesn't seem to be a damn thing I can do about it." And with no more warning than that, he hauled her up on her toes and into his arms and his mouth found hers.

Her lips were cold, and her breath was seemingly caught in her throat. For what seemed like an eternity, she stood motionless in his arms, frozen, hardly breathing. But even through their coats and party clothes, he could feel the tension that wired her and knew that as hard as she tried, she wasn't indifferent to him. Murmuring her name, he gathered her closer and blindly rubbed his mouth against hers, warming her, nuzzling her, slowly, patiently melting her bones.

Her arms trapped against his chest and her senses starting to swim, Rocky fought the sweet, enervating tug of seduction. She couldn't do this, she thought desperately. She *wouldn't!* But no one had ever kissed her the way he did, with all his concentration focused on her. Just her. The wind swirled around them, blowing snow and nipping at every exposed inch of skin, but it might have been the middle of summer for all the notice he gave their surroundings. His arms were snug around her, and his only thought seemed to be pleasuring her. His mouth wooed and caressed and teased, stealing her breath, her common sense, delighting her, until she couldn't think of anything but the hunger he lit in her blood. With a shudder that seemed to come all the way from her toes, she clutched at him, moaning, and kissed him back.

They might have stood there locked in each other's arms, for seconds, or it might have been an eternity—later, she could never be sure. From the clinic parking lot, several of the guests called goodnight to each other, car doors slammed and motors revved to life. Before it even occurred to Rocky that cars were pulling onto the road and turning in their direction, Lucas put her away from him. By the time the headlights picked them out of the night like spotlights, they were a good three feet apart and not even touching.

His eyes as black as midnight and fierce with something that set her heart somersaulting in her breast, he said roughly, "Where're your keys?"

Dazed, she looked up at him blankly. "What?"

The corner of his mouth twitched, then slowly curled into a crooked smile. "Your keys, honey. Where're your keys?"

It was the amusement lacing his words that snapped her back to reality. Suddenly realizing that she was staring up at him like a teenager with a bad case of hero worship, she jerked her eyes down to her hand and the set of truck keys she held. She had no idea how they'd gotten there. Without a word, she handed them to him.

Ten seconds later, he had the door unlocked and her safely installed behind the wheel. As far as Luke was concerned, that was ten seconds too long. What the hell had possessed him to kiss her? He had to get out of there and think, dammit! But after he handed her back her keys, walking away from her wasn't nearly as easy as he'd have liked. In fact, it was damn near impossible. One hand on the roof of the pickup and the other braced on the open door, he frowned down at her. "Are you all right?"

The dazed look had faded quickly from her eyes, or at least he thought it had. She wouldn't quite look at him. Jamming the key into the ignition, she said with a forced lightness, "I'm fine. Why wouldn't I be?"

Lucas could think of a whole host of reasons, not the least of which was this crazy chemistry between the two of them, which didn't seem to thrill her any more than it did him. Dammit, where the hell had it come from? And why couldn't he control it? He'd never had any trouble keeping a tight rein on his emotions before, but with her, he was like a randy kid who'd just discovered what all the fuss about sex was about. He couldn't get enough of her.

But he had no intention of telling her that. If she wanted to pretend that the ground hadn't shifted beneath their feet during that kiss, he was damn well going to let her. Because if he didn't, he'd have no choice but to pull her out of that car and into his arms again and show her just exactly why she couldn't possibly be as all right as she claimed. And then he just might not be able to let her go.

Stepping quickly back, his jaw rigid, he said tightly, "No reason. Thanks for coming. Drive carefully." He shut the door before she could even thank him for inviting her. Seconds later, she drove off, heading for town. Long after her taillights disappeared from view, though, he stared after her, the taste of her still on his tongue. It was, he knew, one he could become addicted to if he wasn't damn careful.

Rocky's first emergency call came in four days later—an injured hunter, Sam Katz, trapped in the mountains with a broken leg and possible spinal injuries. And there was no time to lose. He'd contacted his family with his cellular phone, so weak he could give his wife nothing but vague directions before he passed out. Frantic, Brenda Katz had called Rocky immediately, begging her for help. Rocky had quickly assured her she'd find her husband, but privately the spinal injuries had her worried. That wasn't something she felt comfortable handling alone, not when one wrong move on her part could lead to a lifetime of paralysis for Sam Katz.

So she called around town, trying to find a doctor to go with her, but Clear Springs wasn't exactly overflowing with M.D.s. Three were in surgery, a fourth was out of town at a convention, and a fifth was an OB-GYN who had a patient who was in labor four months early, and he couldn't leave her. That left Lucas.

She didn't want to call him. Not after that kiss at his Christmas party. She'd gone out of her way to avoid him whenever she caught sight of his Bronco in town, and she'd even called Allie to tell her that the man was quietly driving her out of her mind. Far from sympathetic, her sister, blissfully in love with Rafe Stone, had been delighted that she was finally getting over Greg. She'd cheerfully assured her that being crazy about a man wasn't half bad when it was the right man—Rocky should try it some time.

But Rocky had no intention of doing any such thing. If her relationship with Greg had taught her anything, it was that she was a sap when it came to caring about a man. She gave her heart and soul and had nothing left for herself. And that scared her more than she'd admitted to anyone, even Allie. She wouldn't, couldn't chance losing herself again, so she'd deliberately steered clear of Lucas. She had not laid eyes on him since she'd left him standing on the side of the road, and that was just fine with her.

But she needed a doctor, and he was the only one available.

Frustrated, cursing the fickle, irritating whims of fate, she was left with no choice but to call him. All business, she gave him the details as soon as he came on the line, then added, "I don't want to take any chances with a spinal injury, so I need an M.D. to go with me. I know this is short notice, but no one else is available. Can you go?"

If he noticed that she'd asked every other doctor in town before getting around to him, he didn't, thankfully, comment on it. Instead, he asked her what supplies she had on hand, then said, "Give me five minutes to get some things together, and I'll be right there."

He was as good as his word, arriving five minutes later just as Rocky was warming up the chopper. There hadn't been time to go home to change into clothes appropriate for the mountains, so he'd had to content himself with waterproof boots, a down jacket and a ski cap.

"Glad to have you on board, Dr. Greywolf!" Charlie yelled over the roar of the rotors as he took Luke's bag and set it with the thermal blankets, tents and other gear in the back before sliding the cargo door shut. "I don't like the idea of Rocky going up in those mountains all by herself." Glancing past him to Rocky, who couldn't hear anything over the roar of the rotors, he grinned. "But if you tell her I said that, I'll flat-out deny it. In you go, Doctor. Don't forget to buckle up. It's probably going to be a wild ride."

Wild didn't begin to describe the flight that followed. Within seconds of strapping into the seat next to Rocky, he learned that everything he'd heard about the little daredevil was true. The cockpit door was slammed, she looked to Charlie for a thumbs-up signal and took off at a speed that left Lucas's stomach back on the ground. He half expected her to laugh, but she didn't even spare him a glance. Her expression more somber than he'd ever seen it, she cut sharply toward the snow-covered mountains in the distance, her eyes on the horizon as she held out a pair of earphones to him that were identical to the ones she was wearing.

"From what I could make out from Mrs. Katz, Sam's somewhere on the eastern slope, near the tree line," she said as he tugged the headgear into place. "There're binoculars under your seat. Keep an eye out for a splash of orange. Sam took an orange hunting vest with him, but his wife wasn't sure if he was wearing it when he fell."

Immediately reaching for the binoculars, Luke followed her gaze to the horizon and the mountains they were racing toward. Shrouded in dark blue-gray clouds, the peaks lost to view, they looked cold and forbidding and dangerous. "What's the forecast?" he asked, frowning. "Isn't there another front coming through?"

She nodded, her hands easy on the controls. "It wasn't supposed to get here until in the morning, but the weather service updated the forecast right before we took off and now expect it well before midnight. That looks like the leading edge of it."

She didn't have to say that the cold front's early arrival made the situation ten times worse—they both knew it. An injured, vulnerable man, separated from his companions and alone in the mountains with no one to help him was prey not only to whatever wild animal came along, but also to the weather itself. If he was out in the open, exposed to the wind and the snow, the below-freezing temperatures that were sure to come with the advancing of night could spell disaster. If they were going to find him—and save him—they had to do it soon. His face grim, Lucas brought the binoculars to his eyes and studied the tree line for a flash of color.

It was like looking for a needle in a haystack from a swing. Rocky kept the helicopter as steady as possible in the winds that whipped around the mountains' higher elevations, but as she swept up and down the tree line, the sensation was a lot like swinging. Then it began to snow.

Rocky swore at the fat wet flakes that swirled around them, obscuring the rocky, jagged mountain below, and threw Lucas a quick glance before bringing her attention to the white scene spread out in front of the windshield. "I'm going to have to take it down to the treetops, or we're not going to be able to see squat. Hang on."

In the time it took to blink, they dropped two hundred feet, until they were just a stone's throw from the top of the pines that stubbornly clung to the steep terrain. Through the thick white clouds of blowing snow, they could just make out the sharp, jagged rocks below, the thinning trees, and very little else. Aside from the pines, there wasn't a spot of color anywhere. Or a single sign of life.

"I don't see a damn thing," Lucas growled into the mike attached to his headphones. "Are you sure the wife said he was on the eastern slope of the range?"

Rocky nodded, her eyes, like Lucas's, locked on the cold, barren scene below. "She said he always hunts around Bighorn Lake every year, so we're in the right spot. He's got to be around here somewhere."

"A hunter can cover a lot of territory. He could have wandered miles from the lake without realizing it before he fell, especially if it was snowing this hard. It's damn near white-out conditions, and all the landmarks look alike. Even someone familiar with these mountains could get disoriented—it happens nearly every hunting season. Let's try farther north."

A simple movement of her hand on the control stick took them deeper into the mountains, and for long, endless moments there was nothing but the sound of the rotors overhead beating the silence as they scoured the countryside with unblinking eyes. Nothing moved, however, except the whirling snow.

And with every passing second, the odds were growing against their finding Sam Katz. They were running out of daylight, and the storm was intensifying, destroying what little visibility there was. If they didn't find Katz damn soon, they were going to have to call it quits for the day and try again tomorrow. And by then it would probably be too late.

"There!" Lucas suddenly exclaimed, pointing to a spot off to the east. "Near the base of that rockslide. I thought I saw something."

Afraid to hope, Rocky swung sharply to the right and raced toward the slide, which was a deep, snow-covered gouge in the earth. Hovering as close as she dared, she frantically searched below them. "Where? I don't see anything but rocks—"

Leaning forward in growing excitement, Lucas pointed a hundred yards in front of them. "There, by that fallen pine. There's something orange under the branches. See? And it's moving! That's him! He's waving at us!"

It was a weak wave, but it was definitely a wave. Relieved, Rocky let out the breath she hadn't even realized she was holding, tears, just for an instant, stinging her eyes before she hastily blinked them back. "Thank God, thank God! Hang on while I find a place to set her down. I've got a winch, but in this wind, I don't want to chance it."

Finding a place to land, however, proved to be easier said than done. The terrain was steep and rocky and dotted with trees. "I can't do it," she said, muttering curses under her breath. "Not here. It's too risky. We'll have to go to a lower elevation to find a meadow, then hike back."

"That could take a while, and I don't like the looks of this storm," Lucas said with a frown. "Is there a way I could throw some food and blankets down to him?''

''Yeah, there's a hatch in the floor, halfway back. Hang on while I get in position.''

It only took her seconds to align the helicopter directly over the fallen tree that Sam Katz had managed to crawl under for shelter. At her shout that she was ready, Lucas opened the hatch and threw down three thermal blankets and enough bags of dried fruit and nuts to hold the injured man over until they could get to him. Anticipating the pull of the wind, he'd bundled everything together, weighted it with several cans of evaporated milk Rocky had included with the food items and tied it all together with a piece of rope he found in a storage compartment. Stretched out on his stomach, he watched as the bundle fell like a rock and landed within two feet of the fallen pine.

''Bull's-eye!'' Rocky crowed as Sam Katz flashed them a thumbs-up signal and grabbed the supplies. ''Nice shot, Doc. Now let's find that landing sight.''

Finding a high-country meadow big enough to land the chopper in wasn't that difficult—but making the hike back up the mountain to where they'd had to leave Sam was. It was almost straight up, and the footing was treacherous and icy as the last light of day began to fade. Taking time only to call Charlie on the radio and apprise him of the situation, they started climbing. Loaded down with backpacks, medical supplies and a stretcher, they couldn't move nearly as fast as they needed to.

His lungs burning from the altitude and the strain of the climb, Lucas cast a quick glance over his shoulder to Rocky. Flushed and huffing, she was two steps behind him and showed no signs of slowing down, in spite of the fact that the muscles in her legs, like his, had to be knotted and aching. She had guts, he silently acknowledged. She carried her share of the load and didn't complain. And as much as he hated to admit it, he found that damn attractive.

Seeing his eyes on her, she gasped, "How much farther?"

"Another quarter of a mile. You gonna make it?"

She could hardly draw breath to speak, but she still managed to shoot him a cocky grin. "What do you think?"

Chuckling, he faced forward and continued up the mountain.

They reached Sam Katz ten minutes later. His bearded face pale as death and etched with deep furrows of pain, he lay at an awkward angle under the shelter of the fallen pine, wrapped in the blan-

kets Lucas had dropped to him nearly an hour earlier. The heavily falling snow all but covered him.

"You f-found m-me," he whispered in a voice so
faint it hardly carried over the low moan of the
wind. "I was beginning to think no one w-would."

"You're going to be just fine, Sam," Lucas assured him as he crawled under the tree with him and
unobtrusively took his pulse while he introduced
himself and Rocky. "I understand from your wife
that you've got a broken leg and possible spinal injuries, so you just lie still and let us take care of
you. We'll have you warm and dry and feeling better in no time."

"Tell me what you need," Rocky told Lucas
quietly as she turned on a small but powerful fluo-
rescent lantern and positioned it under the tree near
where he knelt next to the injured Sam. In the sudden bright light, the hunter barely had the strength
to lift his arm and cover his eyes.

"My bag, the backboard and the stretcher,"
Lucas murmured. "I need to get that leg set and
immobilize him before we see what we can do about
this damn tree."

"You just take care of him," Rocky replied as
she retrieved the things he'd asked for. "I'll deal
with the tree."

Lucas didn't believe for a second that she could
move it by herself, but his more immediate prob-

lem was his patient. Besides his more obvious injuries, he was suffering from exposure and dehydration and shock. If they didn't soon get him out of the weather and get some fluids in him, Sam Katz was going to be in more trouble than he already was. Cursing the snow that continued to fall at an alarming rate, Lucas went to work.

When he glanced up again, it was to discover that Rocky had brought along a small hatchet and chopped enough of the dead tree away to allow him to slide Sam out from under it on the stretcher. The corners of his mouth twitching, he murmured, "You never cease to amaze me, Ms. Fortune. Next time I need some firewood, remind me to call you."

He expected her to grin and toss back a saucy remark, but she didn't so much as crack a smile. "We've got a problem," she said in a low voice. "There's no way in hell we're going to get off the side of this mountain tonight . . . not with the way things have started to ice up the last fifteen minutes. It's just too dangerous. Even if we could make it back to the chopper in the dark without falling and breaking all our necks—and that's a big if— flying would be a real crapshoot."

Glancing around, Lucas had to admit she was right. He'd been so wrapped up in his patient that he hadn't noticed the worsening weather conditions. The snow that had been falling at a steady rate for well over an hour was now mixed with sleet that was quickly coating everything with a gradually thickening layer of ice.

"Damn! Then we'd better leave Sam right where he is until we get some type of shelter put together—"

"Camp," the other man said hoarsely, struggling up out of the light doze he'd slipped into. "I've got a camp set up...j-just over there." His neck encased in a neck brace, he glanced to the trees off to the left, the last of his energy flagging as he whispered, "Couldn't m-make it..."

Pulling another flashlight from her pack, Rocky said, "I'll check it out," and slipped off into the dark. Within seconds, she was back, her smile relieved. "It must be our lucky night. He's got a tent and a down sleeping bag just waiting for him about a hundred yards into those trees."

"Then let's get him moved," Lucas said as he moved to the head of the stretcher and began to push it clear of the few branches that Rocky hadn't hacked away. "Easy. That's it. We need to carry him if possible—I don't want to jostle him by sliding the stretcher all the way to his camp if I can help it. Think you can handle his feet?"

Sam Katz wasn't a big man, thankfully, but Rocky didn't fool herself into thinking he was a featherweight. He might not be muscle-bound, but he was solid and outweighed her by a good thirty or more pounds. Studying him, she nodded grimly. "I might have to stop every twenty yards or so, but, yeah, I can do it." Moving to the foot of the stretcher, she squatted and got a good grip. "One...two...*three!*"

Twenty minutes later, standing outside the small one-man tent they'd just eased Sam into, Rocky watched as Luke disappeared inside the narrow space to make sure the hunter would be comfortable for the night and found herself confronted with another problem. When she hurriedly packed for this rescue attempt, she'd thought she'd brought along everything she would need for any emergency that might crop up. But she'd never expected to spend the night. She'd included one tent, one that was almost a carbon copy of Sam's, in her backpack as a precaution, in case Lucas needed a dry, sheltered area in which to treat Sam's injuries. And now she was going to have to share that same tent with the doc.

Her heart did a slow slide into her stomach at the thought. Hugging herself, she reminded herself she was a professional. And so was Lucas. They were only up here at the top of the world because of their work, and the situation was hardly romantic. In fact, she couldn't remember the last time she'd been trapped in such miserable conditions. She was cold and hungry and tired, and her clothes were wet. She'd called Charlie on Sam's cellular to let him know about the change of plans, and all she wanted to do now was find a place out of the wind, dry out, then get some sleep. And to do that, she had to set up the tent. Her chin set with resolve, she went to work.

Ten minutes later, she was finished. Luckily, they'd brought enough thermal blankets for an army, so there would be plenty of covers to keep them warm. Her hands on her hips, her frown directed at the tent, which seemed to get smaller every time she looked at it, she let out a wistful sigh. She'd feel a whole lot better if the dang thing was about three times bigger. The way it was, one of them wouldn't be able to move so much as an eyelash without the other one feeling it.

Lost in thought, she never saw Lucas ease his wide shoulders through the opening of Sam's tent and crawl out. Suddenly he was standing behind her and watching her with a quizzical frown. "Problems?"

Startled, she whirled to find him less than four feet behind her, his knowing eyes seeing far too much. "No! I mean yes!" Hot color surged into her cheeks, mortifying her. Dragging in a calming breath, she let it out in a huff and forced a smile that was more than a little strained. "What I mean is that I didn't exactly plan for a sleepover in the mountains, so this will have to do." Grimacing, she turned her attention back to the tent—the very *tiny* tent, she realized now that she'd gotten another look at Lucas's shoulders. "Please tell me it's bigger than a sardine can."

"It's bigger than a sardine can," he repeated obediently, then ruined the effect by adding with a grin, "if you're a shrimp. Are you actually planning on both of us sleeping in that thing?"

"I don't see that we have much option . . . unless you want to bunk with Sam," she added hopefully.

"And chance bumping him in my sleep? I don't think so."

Somehow she'd had a feeling he'd say that. Giving in graciously to the inevitable, she sighed in defeat. "Then I guess it's just you and me, Doc. You want the right side or the left? It makes no difference to me."

He chose the left, but instead of following her inside as she expected, he squatted down on his haunches in front of the tent opening and peered in at her. "I'll be right back—I'm going to check on Sam one more time. While I'm doing that, you can get out of those wet clothes."

Four

"I can *what?*"

"Strip," he said flatly. "And don't even think about giving me an argument on this, lady. Your clothes are wet, and so are mine. The last thing we need right now is frostbite."

"But—"

"You've got five minutes, Rocky. I suggest you don't waste them."

Outraged temper flashed in her eyes, but before she could tell him what he could do with his five minutes, he was gone, letting the tent flap fall shut behind him. Of all the incredible nerve! she fumed. Who did he think he was, ordering her around as if she were some kind of kid who didn't know when to come in from the rain? Strip, indeed! She'd strip when she was good and ready, and not until then.

You do that, Miss Hoity-toity, a needling voice drawled in her head. *You wait long enough, and the doc'll be back to enjoy the show. Is that what you want?*

Her heart rolled over in her chest at the thought, heated images playing before her eyes.... Lucas crowding into the tent with her, his brown eyes nearly black as he watched her slowly remove her clothes, piece by piece, with fingers that trembled. He wouldn't touch her—not at first, anyway—but he wouldn't have to. The stroke of those wolfish eyes of his would be as physical as a caress. Before he ever laid a hand on her, she would be seduced.

Was that what she wanted? To be seduced by Lucas Greywolf?

Instinctively she immediately rejected the idea, but deep inside a pulse quickened with expectation. Dismayed, she stiffened. No, she thought firmly. He'd just caught her off guard, that was all. She hadn't planned on spending the night in the mountains at all, let alone in a one-man tent with Lucas. And naked, at that! Add the memory of a couple of scorching kisses to that scenario, and it was no wonder she was being fanciful.

"He didn't tell you to strip because he plans to ravage you," she muttered to herself in disgust. "It was strictly for health reasons, so this is no time to act like an outraged virgin. You keep this all business, and he will, too. So get out of your damn clothes and under the covers before he gets back!"

Casting a quick eye to the tent entrance, she wondered how long he had been gone and hurriedly began to shed her damp clothes. Shivering, her fingers far from steady, she hesitated when she got to her bra and panties, reluctant to take them off. But they were damp from the moisture that had seeped through the rest of her clothes, and with a resigned sigh she tugged them off, then scrambled under the covers. She'd hardly settled onto her side of the tent and switched off the flashlight before Lucas was back and easing inside.

Lying with her back to him, the covers pulled all the way up to her ears, she clung to her side, but there just wasn't enough room for the two of them in the small tent. His arm brushed her shoulder, his hip nudged hers, and suddenly she couldn't breathe without dragging in the scent of him. Going perfectly still, she found herself waiting for the next innocent touch. But it was the growling of his zipper that accosted her senses next, then the rustle of his pants as he tugged them off.

Her heart slammed against her ribs, and between one heartbeat and the next, her mouth went as dry as dust. *Don't be a ninny,* she ordered herself sternly. But it was already too late. Professional or not, there was no way she could lie there and pretend indifference while a man peeled out of his clothes right next to her. Especially when that man was Luke Greywolf. With every article of clothing he removed, she found it harder and harder to think of anything except that. He was spending the night with her in the buff. How, dear God, was she supposed to even think about sleeping?

Her senses spinning, she never heard him finish undressing, but suddenly he was stretching out beside her under the covers. Silence engulfed them, as thick and tangible as a creeping fog, while outside the wind moaned and howled and threw snow against the nylon walls of the tent. It was a cold sound, and unbearably lonely. Behind her, she felt Lucas's body heat scorching her back, warming her all the way to her toes. Her fingers curling into fists in the blanket as she clutched it to her like a shield, it was all she could do not to roll back and snuggle up against him.

Rocky never knew how long they lay like that, stiff and unmoving, waiting for something neither of them wanted to acknowledge. Her heart jerking in her breast, her nerve endings starting to tremble from the strain, she willed herself to relax, but she was as rigid and unbending as an old maid who had never known a man's touch.

Finally, unable to stand the silence another second, she blurted out, "Do you think the snow'll stop by morning?"

The question was like a shout in the darkness, shattering the tense, intimate quiet. A second passed, then another, before Luke said in a rough voice, "It should blow itself out by morning, especially with this wind."

Silence fell again, thicker than before. Shifting restlessly, Rocky said, "I guess you spent a lot of time in these mountains as a kid, huh?"

"How did you know I grew up here?"

Surprised that he even had to ask, she said, "Are you kidding? According to the grapevine, you're the greatest thing since sliced bread around here. Not only did you actually make it off the reservation and all the way through medical school, you came back. Apparently most people don't."

"I'm not most people." Lying on his side, facing her, her scent surrounding him and slowly driving him out of his mind, Lucas would have sworn he had no intention of discussing his past with her. But the night and the intimacy of their surroundings invited confidences, and without quite realizing how it happened, he found himself telling her about a childhood spent exploring the forests and streams that his ancestors had claimed as their own and about the hold the land had on his heart. A hold that he hadn't even realized was there until he went away to college and found himself miserable with homesickness. He hadn't come back for any altruistic reasons, at least not any he was willing to discuss with her, but simply because he had no other choice. He hadn't been able to stay away.

"So you came back home and got married and set up your practice," she said quietly. "Was your wife from here, also, or someone you met in college?"

Not surprised that she knew about Jan—the local matchmakers had probably told her the story her first day in town—he flinched at the images that flashed before his mind's eye. Jan, with her dancing eyes and flashing smile, full of sass and vinegar, as daring as the woman who lay beside him. It was her eagerness to experience all that life had to offer that he'd fallen in love with—and the reason he'd lost her. There hadn't been anything she wouldn't try, including mountain climbing. When she'd fallen trying to scale a sheer rocky cliff, all of his medical skills hadn't been enough to put her back together again. He should have been able to do something, but he hadn't, dammit, and he would live with that regret the rest of his life.

"We went to high school together," he said shortly.

"And she waited for you all that time? She must have loved you very much—"

"As much as I loved her," he said curtly, cutting her off. "Losing her was hell, which is why I don't ever intend to love anyone like that again. Now that we've got that cleared up, I suggest we both get some sleep. Tomorrow's going to be a hard day.''

He couldn't have been more blunt if he told her flat out not to get any ideas about him, and Rocky got the message loud and clear. He was still in love with his dead wife.

As if she cared, she thought huffily. He didn't have to worry about her tripping him and beating him to the ground. The last thing she wanted was a no-win competition with a ghost for a man's affection.

But as she mumbled a toneless good-night and scooted as far from him as possible, it wasn't relief that coursed through her, but something that felt an awful lot like disappointment.

Lucas was too conscientious about his patient and too aware of the naked woman beside him to sleep for longer than a few hours at a time. Waking just after midnight, he tugged on his clothes and waded through the drifts that had piled up between the two tents to check on Sam, who was, thankfully, sleeping soundly. As warm as toast in his down sleeping bag and showing no signs of a fever or infection, the hunter didn't so much as blink an eyelash when Lucas checked his vital signs. He was still pale and more than a little haggard, and he was damn lucky to be alive. Satisfied that the sedative he'd given him would keep him comfortable for at least three more hours, Lucas quietly crawled back out into the snow and zipped the tent opening closed.

The wind was still howling, and it cut through his clothes like a knife. Swearing, he slogged through the drifts to his and Rocky's tent and quickly let himself in, dragging the zipper shut behind him the second he was inside, but not before he let in a fair amount of icy wind. Rocky whimpered in her sleep and shifted slightly, unwittingly revealing a bare shoulder. Not stopping to think, Lucas moved to tug the cover up closer around her neck.

He should have let her be—she would eventually have burrowed deeper under the covers—but touching her seemed to be an instinct, one he could no more control than he could the call of the wind. His fingers closed around the blankets, pulling them higher, and in the process the backs of his fingers brushed against skin that was down-soft and temptingly warm. Fascinated, he stared down at her in the dark, unable to draw his hand away.

Later, he couldn't have said when she opened her eyes. One second she was asleep beside him, her lashes dark smudges against cheeks that were still rosy and chapped from the wind, and the next she was blinking up at him sleepily, the beginnings of a slow smile flirting with the edges of her mouth, as

if she had been dreaming of him and was pleas-
antly surprised to wake and find him beside her.

Yeah, right, he almost snorted. If she'd been
dreaming of him, she wouldn't have been smiling.
The lady didn't like him. Oh, she might kiss him
like there was no tomorrow, but that didn't mean a
damn thing. When she really needed somebody she
could count on, she'd called every other doctor in
town to help her before she stooped to calling him.
If that didn't tell him what she thought of him,
nothing else would.

But when she smiled up at him with the hint of a
promise in those sultry eyes of hers, he felt the heat
of it all the way to his toenails.

"Go back to sleep," he said in a voice that was
little more than a sandpaper-rough whisper. "I was
just checking on Sam."

She closed her eyes obediently, but instead of
drifting back into her dreams, as he expected, she
murmured, "You're wet. You need to get out of
those clothes." And before he could stop her, she
reached for the zipper of his jacket.

Like a steel trap, his fingers closed around hers.
"What do you think you're doing?"

It was his low, sexy growl that finally brought
Rocky completely awake. The sleep fogging her
brain lifting abruptly, she blinked, then froze at the
sight of her fingers caught in Lucas's. Her eyes flew

to his, and the heat she saw there almost singed her hair. With agonizing slowness, her heart started to pound.

She should move, jerk her hand back, burrow under the covers and put as much space between them as the confines of the tent would allow. But even as her outraged common sense was shouting orders at her, her fingers moved, but only to tug the tab of the zipper lower. "You said yourself that we need to be careful of frostbite, Doc," she replied in a husky voice she hardly recognized as her own. "I was just helping you get undressed."

Beneath her suddenly sensitive fingertips, she felt his harshly indrawn breath and every word that seemed to rumble from deep in his chest. "I'm not a child, Rocky. When a woman pulls my clothes off, she's usually asking for one thing. If you're not, I suggest you keep your hands to yourself."

Her gaze caught and held by his in the darkness, she stared at him for what seemed like an eternity. Then, slowly, deliberately, she unzipped his jacket the rest of the way and reached for the buttons of his flannel shirt.

A muscle twitching in his jaw, he pulled her hand away until she wasn't touching him at all...but only so that he could pull off the rest of his clothes with a haste he made no attempt to conceal. Then he was diving under the covers and reaching for her, all in one smooth motion that stole her breath. Shuddering as his arms slid around her, she surged against him. "You're cold."

"So warm me," he rasped, and covered her mouth with his.

It was a night for dreams, for fantasies, stolen out of time. Her senses reeling from the taste and feel of him against her, Rocky ran her hands over him, delighted with the chance to explore him to her heart's content. Tomorrow, no doubt, there would be second thoughts, but she would deal with them then. For now, there was nothing but the two of them on top of the world.

Skin against skin. How could she have known that it would take nothing more than that to light a fire between them? Her breasts settled against the hard, unyielding wall of his chest, her legs tangled with his, and with a sweet rush of feeling sparks flared at every point of contact. Entranced, her mouth hot and hungry under his, she slowly trailed her hands across the breadth of his shoulders, down his back and over the curve of his hips, exploring the texture of skin and muscle and the powerful way he was made, loving the feel of him. And everywhere she touched, heat flared under her fingertips.

His breathing low and ragged in the hushed silence of the tent, he tore his mouth from hers and buried it against the pulse hammering at the base of her throat. "You're killing me, honey," he growled when she touched him everywhere but where he burned for her. "I want your hands on me."

She didn't have to ask where. Sliding her hand between their bodies, she closed her fingers around the length of him and gloried in the groan she drew from him. "Like that?"

His teeth gritted against the pleasure of her hesitant caresses, the angles and planes of his face harsh with passion, Lucas stood it as long as he could, then abruptly pulled her hand from him before he went off like a rocket. "Enough!" he said hoarsely, rolling her under him and kissing her fiercely. "You're driving me out of my mind."

"Good." She laughed. "Now you know what it feels like. You've been driving me crazy since the first day I met you."

"Oh, really?" Wicked mischief glinting in his eyes, he made a place for himself between her thighs and slowly, carefully nudged his hardness against the liquid heat of her. "Lady, you ain't seen nothing yet. By the time I'm through with you, you won't remember your name."

It was a threat, a promise, a sweet, sweet declaration of intent that set her heart racing in her chest. Given half a chance, she would have told him that anytime he was within touching distance, she

couldn't remember where she was, not to mention
her name, but he took her mouth in a hot, carnal
kiss then, and the words died unspoken on her
tongue. His hands roamed over her, caressing,
stroking, searching out her secrets, learning what
made her shudder, gasp, cry out in need. Then,
when she was boneless and lost to everything but his
touch, he slowly, deliberately dropped kisses everywhere his hands had been.

Arching under him with a keening cry that
seemed to echo on the wind, she clung to him,
breathless, aching, burning for release. "Lucas!"

"I'm here, honey," he murmured, stoking the
fires in her with his clever tongue. "I'll take care of
you. Just hold on."

She tried, wanting to prolong the pleasure, but
the second he eased into her, filling her, and began
to move, she was lost. She felt herself start to come
undone and couldn't for the life of her remember
her name or his. Shattering, she knew only that
she'd finally found the man she'd been waiting for
all her life. And he still loved his dead wife.

The storm blew itself out some time before dawn,
leaving behind a crystal-clear winter wonderland.
Waking to the bright glare of sunlight on the snow
soon after dawn, the covers tucked under her chin
and her body tired but sated, Rocky didn't have to

look around to know that she was alone. She'd developed a sixth sense where Lucas was concerned, an early-warning system that screamed like a banshee anytime he was within touching distance, and at the moment it was as dead as a doornail, which meant he was checking on Sam again, just as he had several times during the night. And every time he returned to the tent, they'd made love. Dear God, she must have been out of her mind.

How could she have let such a thing happen? she wondered in rising panic. He'd all but warned her not to get any ideas about him, yet the second he touched her, her brain had just evaporated and every self-protective instinct she had had flown right out the window. And that scared her to death. Because she knew that if he crawled through the tent opening right now and reached for her, she would no more be able to resist him than she could stop the rising and setting of the sun.

Pale, she reached for her clothes with fingers that felt as if they would never be steady again. She couldn't let him touch her. Not again, she promised herself. She was too vulnerable where he was concerned, and she didn't understand why. The lessons Greg had taught her were still fresh, still galling. She'd been so infatuated with him that she'd let him control virtually every phase of her life—right down to the amount of blush she wore!—and she hadn't even realized it until it was almost too late. She'd sworn then she'd never get involved with a strong, possessive man again. None of that had mattered, though, last night.

Lucas could hurt her.

She didn't want to admit it, but if their loving last night had proven anything to her, it was that she had no defenses where he was concerned, no common sense. If she made the mistake of letting herself care for him, he could wrap her around his little finger. And that was something she was determined to avoid.

Her jaw set, she finished dressing and laced up her boots. Not expecting to spend the night, she hadn't brought any cosmetics along, let alone a comb. She had to look a fright, but she wasn't trying to impress anyone, least of all Lucas, she reminded herself. In fact, the less he noticed her, the better. Dragging in a bracing breath, she unzipped the tent and crawled out into the morning sunshine.

After the night they'd spent together, she didn't quite know what to expect from him, but it wasn't a curt nod and a coolness that was frosty as the morning air. Standing by the fire he'd built, unshaven and rugged-looking in his jeans and flannel shirt, he didn't even bother with a good-morning. Instead, he tossed her a granola bar and said,

"Breakfast is going to have to be eaten on the run. We need to get Sam out of here—"

"Has his conditioned worsened?"

"No, but it hasn't gotten any better, and it's a rough hike back to the helicopter. I'll get him ready while you collect the gear."

Not giving her time to argue, he turned his back on her and slipped into Sam's tent, but not before he caught the flash of hurt in her brown eyes. His jaw clenching on an oath, he felt like a bastard. He wouldn't have blamed her if she scratched his eyes out. After the night they'd spent together, she had every right to expect something more from him than the cold shoulder, but, dammit, what the hell was he supposed to do? She'd tapped into emotions in him that no woman, including Jan, had ever come close to touching, and he didn't have a problem admitting that he was shaken. The lady packed a powerful punch.

And she was everything that he wasn't. Rich. White. Privileged. She might shun what her family had for now and play at working, but eventually she'd go back to Minnesota and the easy life she'd left behind. And when she did, she wouldn't take a piece of his heart with her.

That's bull, Greywolf, and you know it, his conscience snapped. *You wouldn't give a damn if the lady was purple and paid all her bills with dia-*

monds. Why don't you be honest with yourself and admit your real problem with her? She's a risk-taker, and you can't handle it. You don't want to worry about another madcap woman who takes chances and doesn't know the meaning of fear. You'd be pacing the floor every time she was five minutes late. And God help you if anything happened to her...

His mouth pressed into a thin white line, he tried to shy away from images of that fateful day when his wife's life force had slipped right through his fingers and there hadn't been a damn thing he could do to save her. But memories were funny things. They had a life of their own, and they defied the strongest will. He felt again the stark despair and infuriating helplessness of that day as he'd frantically worked over her broken body, the pain of loss that had slashed at his very soul and still, to this day, hurt. He'd lost a part of himself with Jan's death, a part he'd never get back. And that was something he couldn't—*wouldn't*—risk going through again.

The matter settled, he went about the business of making sure Sam was ready for transport, then, with Rocky's help, carefully eased him and the stretcher that held him, out of the tent. Their packs loaded and strapped onto their backs, they made the long, dangerous hike back to the helicopter without either of them looking the other directly in the eye or speaking a single word that didn't have to do with the rescue operation.

Once they reached the helicopter and got Sam safely loaded inside, the trip back to town took less than thirty minutes. But it was the longest thirty minutes of Rocky's life. With Sam in the back, she and Lucas were virtually alone in the cockpit. His expression stony, Lucas ignored the headphones when she put hers on, telling her without words that he had nothing to say to her. She should have been relieved. She wasn't in the mood for any kind of heart-to-heart, and if he regretted their lovemaking as much as his coolness seemed to indicate, she didn't have to worry about him wanting anything more for her than what they'd already shared. But still it hurt.

When they reached the landing field, Charlie and two paramedics were waiting for them with the ambulance she'd radioed ahead for. Rushing forward when the rotors had barely slowed, the three of them quickly eased the stretcher holding an exhausted Sam out of the chopper and into the ambulance. Before they could slam the rear doors and whisk him off to the hospital, Lucas was crawling into the back of the ambulance with him.

"Okay," he said. "Let's go."

Seconds later, the ambulance was driving off with sirens blaring and lights flashing, and Lucas hadn't even said goodbye.

The tears she hadn't even realized she was fighting stung Rocky's eyes then, threatening to spill over her lashes. Blinking rapidly, she quickly turned back toward the hangar before Charlie could see, but she might as well have saved herself the trouble. The old man had eyes like a hawk.

"Hold your horses right there, boss lady," he said sternly. "You look like hell. What the devil happened up there on that mountain?"

"Nothing—"

He snorted, the rude sound more than expressing his opinion of that. "Yeah, right. If this is the way you look after pulling off a successful rescue, I'd hate to see you after a failed one." Slinging a friendly arm around her shoulders, he said teasingly, "C'mon, kid, tell your Uncle Charlie what's wrong. Maybe I can fix it."

His gruffness she could handle, but the concerned-uncle treatment got to her every time. Though she was touched, she knew that while there wasn't a motor made that he couldn't fix, hearts were something else. Giving him a watery smile, she said, "I'm just tired. Really. It was a rough trip. In fact, if you don't mind, I thought I'd let you hold down the fort while I go home and catch a couple of hours of sleep. I'm bushed."

"That's a good idea," he said, patting her fondly. "Take the rest of the day off—if anything comes up, I'll give you a call. Oh, and before I forget, Allie called about an hour ago and wants you to call her back."

"Did she say what she wanted?"

He shook his head. "No, she just wanted you to call her as soon as you got in."

"It sounds important. Maybe I'd better call her from here." Hurrying into the hangar, she went into her office and quickly punched out her sister's number, worry furrowing her brow because her gut told her something was wrong. She and Allie shared a closeness that no one but another set of twins would understand. They talked at least two or three times a week, regardless of what parts of the world they were currently in, but those calls were always at night, when they had time to chat...unless there was a problem. The last time Allie called her in the middle of the day, they'd lost Kate.

Counting the rings, she gripped the receiver in a white-knuckled grip until the second her sister came on the phone. "What's wrong?"

"Nothing," Allie assured her, chuckling soft. "I just thought you would want to know that sometime within the next couple of hours, you and I are going to become aunts again.''

"Caroline's in labor?'' Relief washed through her, weakening her knees. Collapsing into the chair behind her desk, she couldn't seem to stop grinning at the thought of her older sister becoming a mother. Once, Caroline's only ambition had been to run the family business as well as their father, Jake, did, but that had all changed with the entrance of Nick in her life. He had brought out the feminine side of her and taught her that there was more to life than just work. Ever since she'd found out she was pregnant, she'd been walking on air.

"I thought she wasn't due until after Christmas. Is everything okay?''

"Just fine,'' Allie said. "I knew you were coming home for Christmas, but with the baby coming and everything, I was hoping I could talk you into coming earlier. Like today.''

"Today?"

"Sure. Why not? You were coming on Friday anyway, weren't you? And it's not like you have to make reservations or anything. Just fuel up the Cessna and come on.''

It was a tempting thought, one that Rocky found she couldn't resist. She needed a bath and some sleep, but she suddenly found that she needed her family more . . . and she also needed as much distance as possible between her and Lucas. Making a snap decision, she said, "I think I will. What hospital is Caroline at?"

"Hope General."

"I'll meet you there as soon as I can." Hanging up, she left Charlie getting the Cessna ready and rushed home to pack. Within the hour, she was on her way home.

It was nearly dark by the time Lucas left the hospital. Sam Katz was resting comfortably and would, thankfully, suffer no permanent nerve or spinal damage as a result of his adventure. But it had been close, closer than Lucas liked. If the man had made one wrong move after his fall...if he and Rocky hadn't gotten there when they had...the outcome might have been tragically different.

That—predictably—brought his thoughts back to Rocky, which wasn't surprising. The hours they'd spent together last night were carved in granite in his brain. And whenever he let his guard down, he didn't even have to close his eyes to see her in his arms, every sweet, beautiful inch of her naked and hot and his to touch and explore. Just thinking about it made him hard.

The lady had taken him apart and put him back together again, and it was going to take him more than a little while to deal with that. But he shouldn't have been so short with her, not after what they'd shared. That was inexcusable, and he wouldn't blame her if she hated his guts for it.

He would have to apologize.

His gut twisted in rebellion at the thought—she hadn't exactly been chatty with him, either, and she probably just wanted to be left alone—but putting it off would only make the situation more difficult. His jaw set, he flagged down one of the town's two taxis and hitched a ride back to the airfield.

The place was deserted, however, except for her mechanic, Charlie. "She's not here," the old man told him. "She's gone home to Minneapolis. Flew out of here about two hours ago."

Stunned, Lucas told himself it was for the best. By the time she came back—*if* she came back—he'd have his feelings for the lady all worked out and under control. He should be grateful to her for giving him some space. Instead, he was hurt, and he didn't like it one damn bit.

Five

Stepping off the elevator onto the maternity floor, Rocky stopped short at the sight of the crowd of family milling around the waiting area directly across from the nurses' station. Her older sister, Natalie, was there, along with Allie and Rafe, and Nick, of course, the proud daddy-to-be. Nervously pacing, his dark hair practically standing on end from running his fingers through it, he was clearly a basket case. Totally oblivious of what was going on around him, he walked right past Rocky without even seeing her.

Grinning, she started to tease him, only to have the words slip right out of her head at the sight of the other couple in the waiting room. Her parents were both there... *together* ... in the same building. Stunned, she stopped in her tracks, unable to do anything but stare, while hope flared in her heart.

Please, dear God, let them be back together, she prayed silently. *We could use a miracle or two.*

Ever since her grandmother's sudden death, the family had suffered one blow after another. Kate's loss and the reorganization of the company had caused Fortune Cosmetics stock to take a dive on the stock market, and then a mysterious break-in at the company lab had led to a setback in the development of the company's new Secret Youth Formula. Rocky knew her father had tried to hold it all together, and had, for the most part, managed to succeed. But the cost had been high. Nearly a month ago, he and her mother, Erica, had separated after over thirty years of marriage.

Seeing them together, Rocky desperately wanted to believe they had worked things out, but she could see that her mother was avoiding Jake as if he were some kind of toad that had just crawled out of the mud. If it hadn't been so sad, it would have been comical.

"Rocky!" Allie spotted her then and rushed forward with a huge smile of relief. "Thank God you're here," she said in a low whisper as she hugged her.

"Mother hasn't said two words to Dad since he got here a couple of hours ago," Natalie confided as she, too, hugged her.

"At least she's here," Rocky pointed out quietly. "I would have bet money nothing short of a nuclear disaster could bring those two together in the same room." Drawing back, she grinned as her parents and two brothers-in-law came forward to welcome her home. "So where's that new niece or nephew of mine? I thought everybody would be celebrating by now."

"So did we, dear," her mother said as she embraced her. "The doctor says there's nothing to worry about—the baby's just taking its own sweet time. I can see right now it's going to take after your father, poor thing."

Rocky bit back a grin as her father shot her mother a murderous glance. "I can think of worse traits it could inherit," he retorted. "Like—"

"Now, children, don't fight," Rocky said quickly, chuckling. "Are you holding up okay, Nick? You look a little the worse for wear."

Haggard and pale, he shook his head. "Caroline's in so much pain. And it's all my fault. I swear I'll never touch her again." In a daze, he turned back to the delivery room. "I've got to get back in there. She could need me...."

"Poor devil," Rafe said sympathetically. "If I was in his shoes, I'd be giving the doctor holy hell for not rushing things along."

"You'd be a wreck, and you know it," Allie said, smiling lovingly into his fierce eyes. "Caroline's tough. She's doing just fine."

Rocky watched dark, intimate messages pass from her twin sister's eyes to her husband's, and suddenly, inexplicably, found her thoughts crowded with images of Lucas leaning over her in the darkness of the tent they'd shared in the mountains, his eyes black with passion, his hands slow, knowing, magical. Heat curled in her belly. What was he doing right this very minute? she wondered as something that felt an awful lot like loneliness squeezed her heart. Did he even know she was gone? Would he care when he did?

"Rachel? Are you okay, honey?"

Lost in her thoughts, she looked up to find her mother—and the rest of the family—frowning at her searchingly. Hot color surged like a tide into her fair cheeks. "Of course. I was just...thinking about something else." Deliberately changing the subject, she said, "So somebody fill me in on the latest gossip. What's been going on while I was gone?"

"The stock is still nose-diving," her mother said flatly. "Evidently whatever your father is doing to pull us out of this rut isn't going over very well with the stockholders. They're still jumping ship like passengers on the *Titanic*, right into Monica's waiting arms."

Rocky winced at the mere mention of the legendary screen star Monica Malone. Famous for her beautiful skin, she'd endorsed Fortune Cosmetics for years, but now, for reasons known only to herself, she was bent on a vengeful takeover of the company. "Kate's probably rolling over in her grave. If we could just get the formula finished, share prices would go through the roof and she wouldn't be able to touch us. What about Mr. Devereax?" she asked.

Hired by the family after Kate's death, Gabriel Devereax was a private investigator with impeccable credentials. "Has he found out anything more about the cause of Kate's plane crash?"

"No," Allie said regretfully, "but at least there haven't been any more break-ins at the lab."

"So the work on the formula is progressing?"

Rafe nodded. "Not as fast as everyone would like, but it's coming along."

Jake started to add that they had high hopes that some of the plants found at the site of the plane wreckage were the ones needed to complete the formula, but his cellular phone rang at that moment, and with a murmured excuse he moved to the end of the hall to answer it. "Hello?"

"I need to see you."

The caller didn't identify herself, but then again, she didn't have to. Monica Malone, even now, when she was well past her prime, had a cool, sexy voice that was still recognizable the world over.

A lesser man might have dropped the phone or at the very least found himself tripping over his tongue. Jake didn't even blink. Turning away so that his family wouldn't overhear any of the conversation, he said coldly, "I don't know how you got this number, but I can't think of a single thing the two of us have to discuss. So if you'll excuse me—"

"What about a little matter of a few hundred thousand shares of stock?" she asked, her voice soft, taunting. "Aren't you the least bit curious about why I bought them? Or what I'm going to do with them?"

He was, of course, but he had no intention of telling her that. "They're your shares, Monica. You can do whatever you like with them."

"Then maybe I'll dump them first thing in the morning, when the market opens. *All* of them," she added sweetly. "Just to see how they tumble."

His mouth grim, Jake just barely swallowed an oath. She'd do it, he thought furiously. Just for the hell of it, she'd start a panic that would send prices right down the toilet. "What do you want, Monica?"

"A meeting with you at my place in twenty minutes," she said smugly. "Don't be late."

"I can't, dammit! I'm at the hospital—my daughter's having a baby."

"That's not my problem. See you, sweetie."

Jake cursed her, but it was already too late. She'd hung up.

"What do you mean, you're *leaving?*" Speaking to him directly for the first time in weeks, Erica looked at him as if he'd lost his mind. "You can't be serious. Caroline hasn't had the baby yet."

"I'm well aware of that," he said curtly. "But something's come up—an unexpected business meeting. I'll be back as soon as I can."

"But surely you can put it off, Dad," Allie said with a frown. "Just for another hour or so. The doctor said it wouldn't be long now."

"And Caroline will be so hurt if you're not here when the baby's born," Rocky pointed out quietly. "Can't you let someone else handle this for you?"

He would have given his right arm to let someone—anyone—take this for him, but he couldn't take the chance. Not with Monica. She was up to something, and he didn't trust anyone but himself to find out what it was. "Not this time," he replied, kissing her cheek, then Allie's and Natalie's. "Tell your sister I'll be back as soon as I can."

He turned then, without sparing Erica a glance, but that didn't stop her from voicing her opinion.

"Don't bother," she muttered bitterly. "Caroline won't need you then."

If Jake heard her, he gave no sign of it. Tall and distinguished, he strode down the hall as if he owned the place and stepped into the elevator. Long after the doors closed and he disappeared from view, Erica silently stared after him with sad, disillusioned eyes.

Giving Rocky a pointed look, Allie motioned her over to the coffeemaker set up in the corner. "They've been this way for weeks now," she said in a low voice. "Snipping and snapping at each other like a couple of kids, with neither one willing to give an inch. We've got to do something."

Rocky agreed. At first she'd tried to convince herself that a temporary separation wasn't necessarily a bad thing. That it might give her parents the space they both needed to realize that their marriage was worth fighting for. But weeks had passed, and the situation obviously wasn't getting any better. If anything, her mother seemed more bitter than ever.

"Why don't you talk to Dad when he gets back, and Nat and I'll see if we can get Mother to cut him some slack," Allie suggested. "Between the three of us, maybe we can make them see reason."

It sounded good, but Rocky only had to look at her mother's set face to know that she and her sisters could talk until they were hoarse, but if her parents weren't ready to resolve their differences one-on-one, they weren't going to get anywhere.

"We can try," she told her sister, "but I don't really think it's going to do much good. This is a husband-and-wife problem, one they have to solve between the two of them, and neither of them seems ready to do that."

Somber, Allie had no choice but to agree.

Monica answered the door to her mansion in the exclusive Lakeview subdivision herself, a slow, triumphant smile spreading across her mouth at the sight of Jake standing impatiently on her front porch. "You came," she purred. "Somehow I thought you would." Stepping back, she motioned him inside, wicked amusement glinting in her famous violet eyes when he hesitated on the threshold. "Contrary to what you may have heard, Jake, I don't bite. Come in...unless, of course, you'd rather have this discussion in full view of anyone who passes on the street. It makes little difference to me. I aim to please."

Jake sincerely doubted that. From what he knew of the lady—and that was using the term loosely— she was demanding and selfish and never pleased anyone but herself. He didn't trust her as far as he could throw her.

He looked her up and down. He'd never seen a woman more decked out for trouble. It was the middle of the afternoon, but she wore silk lounging pajamas and a string of diamonds fit for a queen. And she looked damn good in them. She had to be seventy if she was a day, but her figure was still lush, her hair a natural-looking blond, her face, though finely lined, ageless.

If she'd been anyone else but Monica Malone, Jake might have appreciated her beauty, but she'd caused his family nothing but trouble, and he wanted nothing to do with her. Stepping across the threshold, he waited until she shut the door, then said coldly, "All right, you got me here. What do you want?"

"How about a drink first?" she said easily, crossing the foyer with languid grace to lead him into the formal living room. "What would you like?"

He didn't want a drink. Hell, he didn't even want to be here, but he could see that Monica had her own agenda and wouldn't be rushed. Struggling for patience, Jake sighed and shrugged out of his overcoat. Like it or not, he was going to be here awhile. "Scotch and water."

"That wasn't so difficult, was it?" she said with a sultry smile as she moved to the well-stocked drink cart parked at the end of the couch.

"Please . . . have a seat. Relax. We don't have to be enemies, Jake. All I want to do is talk to you."

Even as he watched her warily, Jake had to give her credit. She was a damn good actress. If he hadn't known she was trying to steal the company right out from under him and his family, he might have believed she was as sweet as Polyanna. What the devil was she up to?

On guard, he avoided the couch and sank down onto one of the French provincial chairs that were invitingly grouped around it. Taking his drink with a curt "Thank you," he said, "Okay, so talk. To what do I owe the honor of this command visit?"

Not the least bit offended, she laughed and sank down on the arm of his chair. "Now, Jake, don't be that way. I didn't actually *command* you to come over here."

She was so close, her hip nudged his arm. Alarm bells clanging in his head, Jake stiffened. Her scent was spicy, exotic, and guaranteed to knock a man out of his shoes. And just that quickly, he knew what she'd called him over here for. Now all he had to do was find out why.

"Let's just say you made it difficult for me to turn you down," he replied, grabbing her hand when she reached out to trail a slender finger down his cheek. Over her ring-laden fingers, his hard eyes locked with hers. "If I didn't know better, I'd say you were flirting with me, Monica. You want to tell me why, or do I have to guess?"

A sexy smile played with the corners of her red lips. "If you have to ask, I must not be doing it right. Isn't the reason obvious, darling? I'm attracted to you."

"Bull." He could have been more diplomatic, but just the thought of her coming on to him turned his stomach. Setting his drink down with a snap on the coffee table, he surged to his feet and put half the length of the room between them with three long strides. His aristocratic features dark with dislike, he turned to face her. "Cut the crap, lady. You have to want something awfully bad to pull this little seduction stunt, so why don't you just cut to the chase and tell me what it is? I haven't got time for this kind of garbage."

Monica didn't so much as flinch, but she could do nothing to stop the flush of hot, embarrassed color that surged into her cheeks. The glint in her violet eyes suddenly hard and ugly, she rose stiffly and faced him with a sinister smile. "If you know what's good for you, you'll take time, darling. One wrong word from me and you could be ruined by sunset."

"And how do you propose to do that?" he retorted. "By going to Erica with this? Go ahead. She might not be talking to me right now, but she knows

I would never do anything to jeopardize the family or the business. And you're a threat to both.''

Reaching for his drink, she said, ''You're damn right I am. You just don't know how much.''

Something in her confident tone made his gut clench. He didn't know what she thought she had on him, but she damn sure didn't sound like she was bluffing. ''Then why don't you tell me?'' he suggested. ''You're obviously dying to.''

She hesitated, pretending to consider, but Jake wasn't fooled. Whatever she thought she knew, she'd called him here to tell him, and there was no way in hell she was going to let him walk out on her without hitting him with it. Finally making up her mind, she sank back down onto the chair he'd just vacated and motioned toward the couch. ''I suggest you sit down, Jake,'' she said flatly. ''You're not going to like this.''

He only snorted. ''Yeah, right. I'll be the judge of that. Just spit it out, for God's sake!''

Her eyes locking with his, she did. ''Ben Fortune wasn't your father.''

''You're lying.''

''Am I?'' she taunted softly. ''Think about it, Jake. Can you honestly stand there and tell me that you never thought about it? Never wondered why you looked nothing like Ben? Or why he always seemed to favor Nathaniel and your sisters over you? For heaven's sake, your birthday's six months after Kate and Ben married. Do you really think he would have waited that long to marry her if she'd been carrying his child?''

Her words hit him like the flicks of a whip, cutting right to the bone. Staring at her, he wanted to yell at her to stop, but deep inside, something cracked...memories, long-forgotten whispers that he'd locked away and refused to examine too closely. A sense that he never quite belonged. A father who loved him but always seemed to be holding a part of himself back.

Dear God, could it really be true? And if Ben wasn't his father, who was?

''His name was Joe Stover,'' Monica said, reading his mind. ''He was a GI killed in the war, before you were born. Now look me in the eye and tell me I'm lying.''

He couldn't, God help him, but he had no intention of letting her see just how shaken he was. ''That's an interesting theory, but I haven't got time for fairy tales right now. If that's all you called me over here for, I've got to get back to the hospital—''

''You walk out that door, and I'll call the press before you reach the street,'' she said icily. ''I mean it, Jake. Tomorrow, headlines all over the country will tell the world that you're not Ben Fortune's son. And that means that you're not his real heir. Nathaniel is, and once he hears about this, he'll walk in and take over, and there won't be a damn thing you can do about it.''

That stopped him in his tracks as nothing else could have. He had no great love for the business and could have walked away from it without a backward glance . . . but not if that meant turning it over to Nathaniel, who had never made any secret of the fact that he thought he could run the company better than Jake did. For as long as Jake could remember, the two of them had competed over everything from who was smarter and the better athlete to who was the more loved by their parents. Just because Kate and Ben—whether he was his real father or not—were now dead, that didn't mean anything had changed.

Reaching for his overcoat so that he wouldn't give in to the temptation to strangle Monica, he turned to face her, his jaw rigid with barely suppressed fury as his gaze met hers. "All right, you've got my attention. I don't know if you're right or wrong, and frankly, I don't give a damn. But the family doesn't need this right now. So what's it going to take to shut you up, Monica? Money? My first born grandchild? Name your price, dammit!''

"Shares, sweetheart," she purred. "I want you to sell me some of your shares in the company."

"Oh, Sterling, look at her!" Kate whispered. "Isn't she beautiful? And they named her after me. Lord, I wish I could hold her."

"Don't even think it," Sterling Foster said in a low, fierce whisper. They were standing in front of the newborn nursery, both of them dressed in surgical greens, complete with caps and masks, and it was all he could do not to haul Kate into the nearest stairwell. He'd done everything but hog-tie her to keep her from coming here, but from the second he told her Caroline had gone into labor, there'd been no reasoning with her. But he couldn't stop trying. As the family lawyer and her friend, it was his duty to watch out for her, even when she thought she could take care of herself.

"Dammit, Kate, we shouldn't even be here. The place is swarming with family. Hell, here comes Rachel—"

Swearing under his breath, he quickly turned his back on Rocky before she could get a good look at him and moved to block Kate from view. But he might as well have saved himself the trouble. A distracted look on her face, Rocky walked right past them without sparing them a glance.

"See." Kate laughed, her blue eyes dancing. "My own granddaughter didn't even recognize me in this getup. Relax. We've got it made in the shade."

He only snorted at that. "In case you've forgotten, someone tried to kill you in that plane crash, and we still don't have a clue who it was. Until we do, you're supposed to be lying low, not paying sneak visits to the newest little Fortune."

Unrepentant, Kate grinned. "Don't scold, Sterling. I just had to see her for myself. Isn't she beautiful?"

Minneapolis was full of lawyers who would have testified that Sterling Foster didn't have a soft bone in his body—whenever a foe foolishly showed a weakness, he went for the jugular with a skill that even his enemies couldn't help but admire. But when his penetrating blue eyes landed on the newest baby in the clan that was his adopted family, there was a definite softness. "She's the spitting image of her great-grandmother. Now can we get out of here?"

The week before Christmas dragged. No one seemed to have time to get sick, and the few patients who did straggle in were just suffering from colds and allergies. Luke treated them and sent them on their way and found himself staring out the window at the hangar where Rocky should have been. Just like a high school kid suffering from his first crush, he thought irritably, turning away. Ever since she'd left, he hadn't been able to stop thinking about her, and he was getting damn disgusted with himself. She was right where she belonged— back in Minnesota with her family, probably in some kind of compound like the one the Kennedys owned, and far above his reach. He didn't care if she ever came back.

Or at least that was what he tried to tell himself over the course of the next few days and nights. But the days were slow, and he had more time than he liked to think. And he found himself thinking a lot about the hot, sweet hours he'd spent with Rocky in a tiny tent in the mountains, the softness of her skin, the way her long legs had wrapped around him....

Cursing, he decided to make some much-needed repairs around the house and clinic while his patient load was low. So he went in two hours early and stayed late at work for three days, painting, then recaulking every window in his house and at the office. And he opened the clinic on Christmas Day.

He tried to convince himself it was just another day, but it didn't feel like one. The silence was deafening. He was restless, and he should have been with family, but his mother had died right after he graduated from high school and his father had never, by his own choice, been a factor in his life. Considering the mood he was in, he didn't want to inflict himself on friends, so while everyone else was feasting on holiday foods, he had a bologna sandwich and chips. He saw a sum total of two patients all day—a pregnant woman suffering from false labor pains and a teenager who had fallen and broken her arm while trying out a new pair of ice skates—and spent the rest of the time trying to find something to do.

By four-thirty, he'd had enough self-torture, and he was just closing up shop when Mary drove up. Dressed in a new bright red sweater and green wool slacks, she took one look at him and started to fuss. "I can't believe you worked. Dammit, Lucas, it's Christmas Day!"

For the first time in what seemed like weeks, he smiled. "People get sick every day of the year, Mary. And you shouldn't be cussing. What would Henry say?"

"That I should have come over here and dragged you by the ear to the house hours ago," she retorted. Bustling around the waiting area, she started switching off the lights. "Get your things. You're coming home with me for a good hot meal. You look like you haven't eaten in days."

"I've been busy. I wasn't hungry."

"And we both know why."

Caught in the act of pulling on his jacket, he sent her a sharp look. "Don't start, Mary. I don't want to hear it."

"Then quit walking around like you lost your best friend," she told him, pushing him out the front door and locking it behind her. "That girl's got you so tied in knots, you can't even see straight. And what do you do? You let her fly out of here like you don't give a damn."

"I don't."

"Horse hockeys! When you get home tonight, take a good hard look in the mirror. If that somber mug of yours is the face of a man who doesn't give a damn, I'm skinny, white and blond."

Lucas laughed—he couldn't help it. "Not in a million years, Littlejohn. Now, if you're through chewing me out, what was that you said about food? I think I could go for a piece of that pecan pie of yours right about now. And a hot cup of coffee."

He was deliberately changing the subject, and they both knew it. For now, though, she was willing to let him get away with it . . . until he needed chewing out again. "You're in luck," she said as she followed him down the steps. "There's one piece left, and it's got your name on it. Let's go."

A few minutes later, Mary served him not only the treasured piece of pie, but also a complete dinner of turkey and dressing and all the fixings that went with it. By the time he finally got out of there and made it home, he was stuffed to the gills and feeling a lot less like Scrooge. For the first time since he and Rocky had made love in that midget of a tent in the mountains, he went to bed and slept like a baby, which was a blessing in disguise. Because the next day, the flu hit.

It rushed through the county—and the reservation—like wildfire, mowing down the old and the young and just about everyone in between who got in its way. Long before his alarm went off, Lucas started getting calls. Leaving Mary to deal with those who could make it into the clinic, he loaded down his Bronco at dawn and hit the road to help those who were too sick to leave their beds.

For over a week, he spent all day, every day, running from one end of the reservation to the other, leaving before sunrise and returning long after dark to a cold, silent house. Somehow, with all she had to do, Mary managed to have a plate of food waiting for him in the refrigerator—all he had to do was heat it up in the microwave. Sometimes he did; other times, he ate it cold and couldn't have said what he was eating. He was too tired to care. Exhausted, he fell into bed at night and never moved again until the alarm went off in the morning.

He lost track of time and never noticed. Then, two days after New Year's, he stopped at a gas station to fill up his Bronco and came face-to-face with Rocky. He hadn't even known she was back.

Stunned, he stared at her like a mountain man who had been too long without a woman. Damn, she looked good. Soft, delicate, feminine right down to toenails that he knew for a fact were buffed and painted. He wasn't a man who cared for fur on a woman, but the white rabbit that lined the hood of her forest-green suede parka contrasted beautifully with her wine-red hair. Her skin would be as soft as that rabbit. And warm. He hadn't forgotten how warm she could be on the coldest night. It was a knowledge that would be with him if he lived to be ninety.

Wondering how she could possibly have gotten prettier in the scant two weeks she'd been away, he shoved his hands into his pockets to keep from reaching for her. "Welcome back," he said coolly. "When'd you get in?"

As polite and distant as he, she shrugged and forced a smile. "A couple of days ago. I hear you've been out single-handedly trying to nip the flu bug in the bud. How's it coming?"

A couple of days! Lucas thought, taking the words like a blow. She'd been here a couple of days, and she was just now getting around to telling him? After the night they'd spent together? If he'd had any time to wonder over the past few weeks just what she thought of him and the lovemaking that had set him back on his heels, he'd just had his answer.

"Fine," he said shortly, suddenly furious. "It's going just fine. Now, if you'll excuse me, I should have been at the north end of the reservation thirty minutes ago. Some of us have to work for a living."

He stalked past her without another word, and he never knew that he'd left her standing there with her mouth open. Staring after him, she said, "What? What'd I say?"

Six

The first three weeks of the New Year, Rocky suddenly found her business taking off like a rocket. A handful of rich college students, looking for adventure before they had to return to school for the spring semester, hired her to fly them into the mountains to ski. Kept busy ferrying them around in search of fresh powder every day for nearly a week, she'd hardly finished with them when a real estate developer with dreams of starting another Aspen hired her to fly him all over western Wyoming, southern Montana, and eastern Idaho. He never did find what he was looking for, but he didn't blame her, and he promised to be back within a month to look for more property.

Not surprisingly, she rarely saw Lucas, which she told herself was just fine with her. The weeks she'd spent with her family over the holidays had given her some time to think, and she was more convinced than ever that a relationship between her and Lucas could never work. He was too much like Greg. And the man didn't even think she worked for a living. That rankled! If she was lonely and her heart contracted every time she did happen to catch a glimpse of him in town, that was just something she'd have to deal with. Some things weren't meant to be.

But she couldn't sleep without dreaming of him, and in the mornings she woke up dragging, her energy nonexistent. She managed to get through the days, but it was only through sheer strength of will. Exhausted, unable to catch up on her sleep, she heard about the flu that was still claiming victims all over the county and had a horrible feeling she was getting it. Charlie, worried about her, grumbled that she needed to see a doctor and nagged at her until she finally agreed.

Because she wanted to see Lucas so badly, she forced herself to go to someone else. A Dr. Hawkins, a grandfatherly type who had a family practice in town, was able to squeeze her in late one Tuesday afternoon. Expecting him to order her to bed with plenty of fluids, Rocky waited patiently for his diagnosis. But when he finally gave it, she couldn't have been more surprised if he'd told her she was slowly turning purple.

"You're pregnant."

Dumbfounded, Rocky could only stare at him. "What?"

A twinkle of amusement glittered in his faded blue eyes. "Obviously you weren't expecting this. You're going to have a baby, Rocky. Your very own bundle of joy. I hope this is good news."

Her mind reeling, she couldn't think. A baby. She was going to have a baby. Lucas's baby. Shock hit her, then joy, swift and fierce, right on its heels. Feeling as if she'd stepped onto a roller coaster that was already flying over the first rise, she started to grin as laughter bubbled up inside her. Lord, how she'd envied Caroline when she held baby Kate for the first time. And now she was going to have a baby of her own. She had to tell the family... and Lucas....

In the split second it took for that thought to register, her joy burst like an overinflated balloon. Lucas, who still loved his dead wife and thought she was nothing but a spoiled little rich girl. Just because she was having his baby, that didn't mean he would ever look at her the way Nick looked at Caroline and Rafe looked at Allie.

"Problems?" Dr. Hawkins asked quietly.

She blinked and came out of her musings to find the doctor quietly watching her. It was the concern in his kind eyes that did her in. She was horrified to find herself suddenly near tears, and she couldn't for the life of her have said why. She was having a baby—alone—and she was thrilled. Defiantly forcing a smile, she said huskily, "It's nothing I can't handle. You just sort of caught me by surprise."

"Then you've got plenty of time to get used to it." He chuckled, patting her shoulder in approval. "Seven and a half months, in fact. You're barely six weeks along."

"And everything's okay? There's nothing wrong? I've been so tired...."

"That goes with the territory," he assured her. "I'm going to give you some prenatal vitamins, and you have to remember that you're eating for two now. That means three squares a day and getting plenty of sleep."

"Can I keep working?"

She'd explained what she did for a living—and the long hours she'd been working—while he examined her. "I don't see why not, at least for right now," he replied. "When you're further along, though, I'm going to have to ground you. You're not going to give me a hard time about that, are you?"

She grinned, knowing herself too well. "I'll probably grumble about it, but by that time, sitting around with my feet up might feel pretty good."

"Good girl." He wrote her a prescription for the vitamins and made a few notations in her file, then rose to his feet. "After you're dressed, stop at the front desk and make an appointment for next month. If you have any problems or questions between now and then, don't hesitate to call me."

"I won't. And thank you, Doctor," she said, with a smile that, though she didn't know it, lit her face with a breathtaking beauty. "I feel like you just gave me the keys to Disneyland."

Laughing, he headed for the door. "Let's hope you still feel that way when your back hurts and the little one keeps you up all night kicking you in the belly. See you in a month."

Her euphoria lasted all the way back to the airfield, until her gaze drifted to where the clinic sat on the far side of the runway. Slowly the light in her eyes faded into bleakness. She was still overjoyed about the baby, but she wasn't kidding herself into thinking that being a single mother was ever what she'd wanted for herself. A baby should have two parents who loved it and each other more than life itself. That was never going to happen with Lucas.

Still, she would have to tell him. It was the only fair thing to do, and he had a right to know. She wouldn't be able to hide it from him much longer, anyway, not unless she intended to go back to Minnesota to have the baby. And that wasn't something she was prepared to do. Clear Springs was her home now. Her business was here, as well as her baby's father. How could she even think about leaving? She would tell him late that afternoon, she decided. He usually closed the clinic around six, and she would catch him before he went home for the night.

But when she arrived at the clinic five minutes before closing, the parking lot was full. Stepping into the waiting room, she found it packed nearly to the rafters, without a single empty seat. Two babies were crying, and Rocky couldn't blame them. The heater was working overtime, and it was hotter than the devil.

Sweat breaking out on her upper lip, she fanned herself with her hand and wondered if she'd made a mistake coming here at this hour. Tomorrow would be better. In the morning, before the waiting room filled up. In desperate need of some fresh air, she turned toward the exit, but before she could take more than a single step, Mary Littlejohn opened the door that led to the examining rooms and saw her.

"Rocky! I didn't know you were here."

"I was just leaving." Conscious of the fact that every eye in the room was watching her curiously, she said, "I don't have an appointment or anything, so I'll just come back later. Maybe tomorrow..."

"No, don't go. Please," the older woman said with a smile. "I know Lucas would want to see you." Turning to an elderly Shoshone woman who was wrapped tight in a waterproof jacket in spite of the heat, she said, "You can go on in, Mrs. Crow. Room two. Dr. Greywolf will be right with you."

That left an empty seat for Rocky, one that she couldn't graciously refuse. Beaming, Mary said, "Sorry about the wait. He'll be with you as soon as he can."

Later, Rocky couldn't have said how long she sat there. It seemed like forever. Within five minutes, she had to get out of her coat, but with the heat so high, she was still sweating. And then there was the constant crying of the babies. One was flushed with fever and couldn't seem to get comfortable, and Rocky's heart broke for it. The other one, a little boy, didn't appear to be sick—he just wanted out of there. And when his pale, drawn, very young mother refused, he threw a tantrum that seemed to echo inside Rocky's head. Her temples starting to throb, she decided she'd had enough and she had to get out of there.

But before she could gather her thoughts enough to collect her things, the door to the back of the clinic open, and suddenly Lucas was standing right in front of her. Just looking up at him made her head swim.

"I just heard you were here," he said quietly, studying her through narrowed eyes. "Are you sick?"

"No! I just needed to talk to you." Everyone in the waiting room seemed to be hanging on her next word. Color climbing into her cheeks, she fumbled for her coat. "I'll just make an appointment and come back another time."

"Don't be ridiculous," he said. "You're already here, and I'll be through within the hour. You can wait in my office."

"That's not necessary," she said, wondering why she'd thought it was so necessary to talk to him today. Grabbing her purse and coat, she jumped to her feet.

She realized her mistake immediately, but it was too late. The room seemed to tilt beneath her feet, and suddenly her head was reeling from the heat and the noise. The blood drained from her face in a rush. Darkness came crashing down on her, and before she could so much as whimper, it swallowed her whole. Without a sound, she started to sink to the floor.

"What the hell?"

Lightning-quick, Lucas snatched her up in his arms, his heart stopping in his chest as her head lolled back against his shoulder. Cursing, he pushed through the swinging door that led to the examining rooms and his office.

When she came to, Rocky found herself lying on the couch in Lucas's office while he leaned over her, his rugged face harsh with worry as he took her pulse. Mortified, she wanted to sink through the floor. "I can't believe I did that," she moaned. "I've never passed out in my life."

"You're sick, aren't you?" he said accusingly. "Dammit, I knew something wasn't right! You're pale as a ghost, and you look like you'd blow away in a good stiff wind." All business, he adjusted his stethoscope around the strong column of his neck and reached for the buttons of her flannel shirt. "What's wrong? Is it the flu? The way you run yourself working day and night, I'm surprised you haven't gotten it sooner. Do you even take time to eat anymore? You must have lost ten pounds, and it was ten you couldn't afford to lose."

"I'll gain it back soon enough," she retorted wryly, grabbing at his hand before he could insert the stethoscope under her shirt. "Lucas, I don't have the flu."

"I'll be the judge of that. I'm the doctor here— you stick to planes and helicopters. Now let go of the stethoscope like a good little girl so I can listen to your heart and lungs."

"There's no need to listen to them. I already went to someone else this morning—"

"Another doctor?" he growled, stiffening, something that looked an awful lot like hurt flashing in his dark eyes. "Who?"

"Dr. Hawkins."

"You went all the way into town when I'm right here?" he demanded incredulously. "Why, dammit? Did you think because of what happened up in the mountains that you couldn't trust me to take care of you?"

"No, of course not. But you weren't exactly thrilled to see me when we ran into each other in town the other day. I thought it would be better if I saw somebody else." From his snarled curse, it was obvious that she was botching this badly, but her tongue seemed to be twisted in knots and the words just wouldn't come "You couldn't treat me, anyway."

"Why not? Dammit, Rocky, if you don't tell me right this second what's wrong with you, I'm going to call old man Hawkins myself and find out what his diagnosis is! And don't think he won't tell me. We go way back—"

"I'm pregnant."

She blurted the words out without finesse, then guiltily rushed to fill the stunned silence with words. "I know you weren't expecting this, and neither was I. It just...happened. Neither one of us was thinking—'' Quickly steering away from that, she assured him stiffly, "I just wanted you to know.... I mean, since we're both living right here in the same town and working within a stone's throw of each other, I thought it was only fair...it's your child, but you're not beholden in any way—''

"Not beholden!'' he echoed, finding his voice at last. "The hell I'm not! What do you mean, you don't expect anything from me? Do you think I'd just abandon you and my baby?''

Caught in the trap of suddenly furious eyes, she winced, cursing her foolish tongue. Why didn't she just shoot herself and get it over with? Struggling to sit up, she floundered for an explanation. "I didn't mean that the way it sounded. This is just all so new, and I don't quite know how to say what I'm thinking. Maybe we both need a little time.''

What Lucas needed more than anything was to put his ear against her stomach and listen for the heartbeat of his child.

The thought came out of nowhere and grabbed him by the throat. A baby. By God, she was having his baby, and it scared the hell out of him. He hadn't planned this—obviously—hadn't even thought of the consequences of making love to her. He'd just wanted her so badly that his teeth ached. He still did. And now there was a baby. His baby.

A child that belonged to him. And he couldn't regret it. Hell, he wanted to shout if from the rooftops...and run for his life. Where the devil did they go from here?

A thousand questions crowding onto his tongue, he wanted to lock the door and keep her there until she answered every one of them. But he couldn't, not when he had sick patients waiting for him out front.

Carefully helping her to her feet, he couldn't bring himself to let her go, not even when it was obvious her dizziness had passed. How could he have forgotten what she felt like under his hands? She was so slender and delicate, almost model-thin. For now, he reminded himself. Soon she would be filling out with his baby. Her breasts would be fuller, more sensitive—

"Lucas?"

Reluctantly jerking back from the tantalizing image, he swallowed thickly. "Look, why don't I come over to your place after work, and we can talk without having to worry about interruptions? I'll wrap things up here in another hour or so and meet you there. Okay?"

"There's no hurry on this, Lucas. I don't want you to feel like you have to... If you have plans..."

"I'm not doing anything but spending the evening with you," he said quietly. "And just for the

record, even if I did have plans—which I don't—
nothing is more important than this.''

Leaving her to chew over that, he made sure she
didn't need him to call Charlie to drive her home,
then returned to his patients.

Concentrating after that, however, was impossible. He treated cold and flu symptoms and an ear
infection, and even stitched up a cut and gave a
tetanus shot with his usual attention to detail, but
his mind was in a fog. Rocky had made it clear that
she didn't expect squat from him where this child
was concerned, but she hadn't said a single word
about how she felt about the baby. Was she scared?
Angry? Ecstatic? Did she even plan to keep it?

His heart stopped at that, dread, like an icy fog,
creeping through his veins. Of course she would
keep it! The Fortunes were big on family—he just
couldn't see her giving away her own flesh and
blood. After all, even if he wanted no part of the
child, she was more than capable of supporting it
on her own. But that wasn't going to be necessary,
he vowed grimly. His child would have the security
of knowing who its parents were and would love
them both. And that meant marriage.

The idea should have rocked him to the core, but
from the moment she'd told him she was pregnant,
he'd known that marriage was the only acceptable
solution to the problem. He didn't try to convince

himself it was going to be easy. She was impulsive, without fear, too used to doing what she wanted without answering to anyone. He could already feel his hair turning gray and knew he had to be crazy to even consider asking her to marry him. But she was carrying his child. And every time they touched, they generated enough sparks to set fire to every forest in Wyoming. A lot of marriages had a lot less than that going for them.

He'd propose tonight.

"You going to stand there all night with that frown on your face or go home?" Mary teased when she bustled into his office and found him staring off into space like a man who had been struck over the head. "The last patient went home ten minutes ago." Suddenly frowning in concern, she felt his forehead for a fever. "Are you okay? You've been acting weird ever since Rocky left. You're not coming down with the flu, are you? Maybe you should come by the house and get some of that chicken soup I made yesterday."

"Chicken soup won't cure what I've got, Mary," he said grimly. "But thanks for the offer. I'll take a rain check, okay? Right now, I've got to get to town. I've got some things to do...."

"What kind of things? Darn it, Lucas, should you be driving? At least take your coat," she called after him as he headed for the door. "It's freezing outside!"

If he heard her, he gave no sign of it. Giving her a distracted wave, he walked out, then had to come back for his keys. Mary hurried to hand him his coat, and she was still shaking her head when he drove off.

When Rocky answered the firm knock at her door two hours after she'd left Lucas's office, she found herself staring at a huge bouquet of red roses that must have cost the earth. They were beautiful, with a scent that immediately brought spring into the small house she'd rented not far from the air field, but she could only stare at them in dismay. She only had to look at Lucas's face and see the glint of determination in his dark eyes to know that he'd gotten the wrong idea. He'd come here to make up and get back together with her. She knew it as surely as she knew she wanted his baby with all her heart. But she couldn't let him do that.

Taking the flowers with a husky "Thank you," she hurried to cut him off. "I'm glad you're here. I've been giving this a lot of thought—"

He cut in as he stepped inside and shrugged out of his coat. "So have I. I need to talk to you. How are you feeling?"

"Fine. Lucas—"

He steered her toward the couch before she could manage anything else and eased her down, then turned to put another log on the fire she already had burning in the fireplace. Seconds later, when he turned to face her, his jaw was set, his eyes penetrating as they swept over her, pinning her to the couch. "You want anything? Something to drink? A pillow for your back?"

"No, really, I'm fine. Lucas, about the baby..."

"The baby's going to be fine," he assured her. "I'll admit you really threw me for a loop, but now that I've had a little time to think about it, I know the two of us can handle this just fine. We'll get married, of course. I'll see about getting the license tomorrow—"

"Married?" He wanted to *marry* her? Stunned, she stared up at him, her eyes searching his in confusion. "But—"

Anticipating her objections, he said quickly, "We can make it work. There wouldn't be a baby in the first place if we could keep our hands off each other, so it's not as if we're indifferent to each other. And a baby needs the security of two parents who live together."

"In an ideal world, yes, of course. But—"

"And it's not like we're a bunch of hot teenagers who don't even know what we want out of life," he continued easily. "My practice is established, and you've got the flying service. You'll have to hire another pilot to take over for you—you can't be flying all over the countryside taking chances when you've got a baby to take care of—but that shouldn't be a problem. Talk to Charlie. He may know someone.''

Caught up in his plans, he talked about buying some land on the edge of town and building a log cabin. There'd be a fireplace in the family room and one in their bedroom, and the rooms would be big and airy and perfect for a child. And dogs. He wanted his kid to have a dog. He'd never had one when he was growing up and every child should have a puppy. And a swing set.

Stiffening, Rocky listened to him make plans that affected not only the baby, but *her,* without once consulting her, and felt resentment flare and ignite deep inside. Dear God, he sounded like Greg! They weren't even married yet, and he was already telling her she had to give up flying. How long would it be before he started telling her when she could leave the house or get out of bed?

''No,'' she said flatly.

Glancing down at her, he grinned in disbelief. ''No? You don't want the baby to have a swing set? But why not? I don't mean right now—''

Pushing up from the couch, she faced him head on, torn more than she had ever been in her life. The life he described sounded like heaven, and with very little effort at all, she could see herself sharing it with him and their baby. But she wouldn't be happy there for long. Not if he was constantly trying to mold herself into the type of wife and mother he thought she should be. They'd both be miserable.

Lifting her chin, she stood straight and proud before him. "I'm sorry, Lucas, but no, I won't marry you."

She expected him to rage at her, and was half prepared for the cutting edge of his tongue. Instead, he waved her answer aside as if she couldn't possibly be serious. "I know it's a big step, sweetheart, but there's no reason to be scared. We'll get through it together."

He started toward her, but she neatly evaded his touch and stepped past him, placing the couch between them. "I'm not scared," she said stiffly. "Or desperate or afraid of being a single parent. I didn't tell you about the baby in the hope you would propose. In fact, I was sure you wouldn't."

That got his attention. His brows jerking together in a scowl, he growled, "Why the hell not?"

"Because you're still in love with Jan," she said bluntly, "and I'm not into threesomes."

The words hit him in the chest like a clenched fist, right in the heart. Stunned, he opened his mouth to deny the outrageous accusation—but there was more than a grain of truth in her words. He did still love Jan. A part of him always would. She was a precious part of his past and those special years when he'd been young and idealistic and thought he could conquer the world and right all its wrongs. She'd been a part of that dream, and when she died, he'd thought he couldn't go on living. But he had, and with each passing year her face and laughter had grown dimmer and dimmer in his memory. She was the past. Rocky and his baby were the future. Somehow he had to find a way to convince her of that.

"Jan is dead," he said stiffly. "I accepted that a long time ago. She has nothing to do with you and me."

She laughed at that, but the sound held little humor. "You can't honestly believe that. I know how she died, Lucas, how you fought to save her. You said yourself you were never going to go through that again. Why would you want to marry me considering all that?"

"You're pregnant. That changes things."

"But don't you see?" she cried. "It shouldn't! You're only proposing out of guilt, and you'll end up resenting both me and the baby. And it isn't necessary. You don't have to marry me to be a part of the baby's life.''

Lucas couldn't believe she was serious, but one look at the stubborn jut of her jaw and he knew she meant every word. She was going to do this, have his baby alone and raise it by herself when she didn't have to. And in the process, she was going to deny him all the little intimate moments that a man and wife shared when they were expecting a child. Oh, sure, she'd let him see the baby when it came, but he didn't want to be just a part of the baby's life—he wanted to be part of *hers*.

Staggered by that, he stared at her as if he had never seen her before. He should have seen it coming, should have realized, he thought numbly. From the first moment he'd laid eyes on the lady, she'd tied him in knots with an ease that thoroughly mystified him. God, he wanted her. It still stunned him how much. They didn't have a damn thing in common expect the baby they'd created, but somehow he knew they were meant to be together.

"Maybe not," he agreed huskily, surprising her. "But my parents weren't married. I don't want that for my child." The admission didn't come easily, and this wasn't something he wanted to talk about. He just knew he'd move heaven and earth to make sure his son or daughter never wondered why his father didn't care enough about his own child to give him his name and marry his mother. "We can work this out. Just because I said I didn't plan to get married again, that doesn't mean I'm still stuck on Jan."

"It's not just that."

Struggling for patience, Lucas reminded himself that her hormones were all over the place and she was entitled to be a little argumentative. He'd just have to handle her with tender loving care and remember that this was all new to her, too. If she tromped on his ego a little bit looking for an excuse not to marry him, he could handle it.

But first he had to touch her. Giving into the need, he stepped around the couch and pulled her into his arms. "Okay, then what is it? Give it to me straight. I'm too tall, my feet are too big, you don't like my favorite color. Tell me," he coaxed softly. "Whatever it is, I swear I'll try to fix it if it's humanly possible. But first you've got to tell me what the problem is."

Wrapped in his arms and standing that close to him, Rocky found it increasingly difficult to hang on to her objections. It would be so easy to say yes and let him play the big strong man to her little woman. But she'd lose herself in that role, and that was too high a price for what he was asking.

"No!" Panic rising in her, threatening to choke her, she fought her way out of his arms. "How can you fix it? You don't even like who or what I am!"

Caught off guard, he let her go. "That's not true."

"Isn't it? You'd fight anybody who demanded you quit medicine, but I'm supposed to quit flying—not only while I'm pregnant, but for *years*—because I can't be running all over creation when I have a child to take care of. And I won't do it, dammit! I let one man try to control my life and promised myself I'd never get into that kind of relationship again. So don't even think about trying to put a leash on me, Doc. Do you hear me? I'm going to fly until Dr. Hawkins tells me I can't before the baby's born, then every chance I get afterward."

"The hell you are!" Jealous—what man?—he glared at her, just daring her to argue with him. "We'll discuss afterward when the time comes, but as long as you're pregnant with my baby, you're grounded, lady. Get used to it."

It was the wrong thing to say. Her chin set stubbornly, she marched to the front door and snatched it open. "You're not my father, Lucas. And I'm not a little girl. Just because I'm carrying your baby, that doesn't mean I answer to you. Now, if you'll excuse me, I think you'd better go. I'm tired and I'd like to go to bed. Alone."

Seven

She was the hardheadedest, most obstinate and infuriating woman he'd ever had the misfortune to tangle with. As he struggled to hang on to his temper, it was all he could do not to grab her and shake some sense into her, then demand some answers about this man he was just now hearing about. She was everything he'd thought she was the second he first laid eyes on her—spoiled and headstrong and too used to getting her own way, come hell or high water. Some man should have taken her in hand a long time ago instead of letting her run free, and by God, he wasn't above doing it himself.

But as much as he was tempted to dig in his heels and stay as long as it took to settle this, he knew this wasn't the right time for such a discussion. She was pale and drawn and—in spite of the haughty, regal way she was looking down that aquiline nose of hers—exhausted. Too late, he remembered that the news of the baby had been just as much of a shock to her as it had to him, and she was dealing not only with that, but with the changes going on in her body. Changes he was partly responsible for, simply because he hadn't been able to keep his hands off of her.

Frustration warring with guilt, he growled, "All right, I'll go, so you can get some sleep. But this discussion isn't over, Rocky. Not by a long shot."

He stormed out before she could do anything but flash her eyes at him. Too agitated to even think about going home, he drove around for what seemed like hours, and later he couldn't have said where he'd been. Alone in his Bronco with only his thoughts to keep him company, all he could think about was Rocky. The way she'd looked when he made love to her, the feel of her under him, surrounding him, the heat that always seemed to flare between them any time they came within thirty feet of each other. She was like a rash under his skin, a yearning that wouldn't go away. And she was carrying his baby.

Something melted in him at the thought, the wall that he'd erected around his heart after Jan's death cracking into a million pieces. Every principle he had rebelled at the thought of the mother of his baby having his child without his ring on her finger. She—and the baby—were his to take care of. To care for. Now all he had to do was convince her of that. If tonight was any indication of things to come, she was going to fight him every step of the way. It was, he vowed, the light of battle glinting in his eyes, a fight he looked forward to.

Restless, his thoughts chasing themselves in circles in his head, he finally found his way home, but he was still too restless to even think about sleeping. Edgy and keyed-up, he prowled around the house in the dark, trying to picture Rocky there with the baby. All he could see, though, was her face when she'd brought up another man, then ordered him out of her house so that she could go to bed—alone. It was an image that stayed with him all night.

By morning, he was in a bear of a mood. Mary took one look at him when he stalked into the clinic and immediately poured him a mug of coal-black coffee. "Here," she said, pushing it across the front desk at him. "You look like you could use this and maybe a couple of nails to chew on."

He took the coffee and swallowed half of it in a single gulp, nearly scalding his tongue off in the process. "Don't start with me, Mary," he muttered. "Not this morning. I'm not in the mood."

Unperturbed, she merely grinned and settled down for a comfy chat before the clinic opened at eight. "What'd Rocky do this time?"

He hadn't meant to tell her or anyone else, but dammit, a man needed someone to talk to when a woman was driving him out of his mind! "She's pregnant and she won't marry me!"

Surprised, the older woman started to grin. "You're going to be a daddy? Oh, Lucas, that's wonderful!" Sweeping around the counter, she gave him a big hug. "Congratulations! A baby! I think that's wonderful! When's it due? Tell me everything. You must be thrilled—"

"Dammit, Mary, right now I'm madder than hell! Didn't you hear what I said? She won't marry me. She won't even consider it."

"So?"

"So?" he echoed, outraged. "What do you mean, *so?* That's my baby she's carrying, and I've got a right to be a part of its life. But will she listen to reason? Hell, no!"

Roaming around the office like a bear with a thorn in its paw, he grumbled and raged and just barely resisted the urge to throw something. "She's got this crazy idea that I only proposed out of guilt and that I'm still in love with Jan. Can you believe that? I told her that was ridiculous, of course, but she claimed that I didn't even like who and what she was. Have you ever heard of anything so ridiculous? Just because I want her to give up flying? There's a baby involved, for God's sake! *My* baby. Of course I want her on the ground! Is that such an unreasonable request from the father of her baby?"

"That depends on if it was a request or an order."

"Well, of course it was a request," he began indignantly, only to remember his exact phrasing. Color tinged his cheeks. "I think."

Mary grinned knowingly. "I've seen you when you start throwing your weight around, Lucas Greywolf. It's not a pretty sight. No wonder Rocky turned you down flat—I would have done the same thing."

That stopped him in his tracks. He turned on her, his brows snapping into a scowl at the sight of her smile. "Dammit, Mary, this isn't funny! I've got a right to take care of my own kid and its mother."

Undaunted, she only shook her head at him. "How you got to the age of thirty-five without learning a darn thing about women, I'll never know. When you ask a woman to marry you, Lucas, she doesn't want to hear about what a responsibility she is."

"But she's pregnant! And I don't care if she and her family have more money than God, she needs me by her side during this."

"I agree," she retorted easily. "But if you said that sort of thing when you asked her to marry you, she probably thought you were doing it out of a sense of duty, not because you really wanted to be with her and the baby. She needs to know you care,

Lucas. That means hearts and flowers and romance, not a logical list of reasons to get married. Pregnant or not, a woman's got a right to expect those kinds of things when a man is asking her to spend the rest of her life with him."

Feeling like a man who had just been hit over the head with a sledgehammer, Lucas swore under his breath, cursing his own stupidity. She was right. All he'd been thinking about was the need to do the responsible thing and get his ring on her finger so that his baby would carry his name. He hadn't once stopped to think how that would sound to Rocky.

"Damn," he said softly, sinking into one of the waiting room chairs. "I think I blew it. I was so concerned about protecting her from her own recklessness that I didn't even kiss her. She said some jerk tried to control her once before and she'd never get in that kind of situation again. I didn't care for the comparison."

Mary grinned. "I don't imagine you did."

"All right, so I acted like an idiot. But hearts and flowers wouldn't have worked anyway. She doesn't love me."

An eternal optimist, Mary brushed that little problem aside with a wave of her hand. "Maybe right now she doesn't, but she must have feelings for you—she's pregnant with your baby. And I've seen the way you look at her. You're not exactly indifferent to her yourself.''

That struck a little too close to the bone. ''We're not talking about me,'' he growled.

''Of course we are,'' she retorted, grinning. ''And don't give me that steely-eyed look of yours. You asked for my advice, and you're going to get it.'' Blithely ignoring the fact that he really hadn't done any such thing, she proceeded to speak her mind. ''You might not think you're ever going to let yourself love anyone again, but you haven't got any say-so in the matter. Especially where Rocky Fortune is concerned. The lady's already under your skin, and you're under hers. Now all you have to do is fan the flames a little hotter, and nature will take care of itself.''

''Nature's not going to take care of anything. In case you missed the news flash, the lady turned my proposal down flat.''

''So you're going to give up? Just like that? Without a fight?''

''She's pregnant, Mary. What else am I supposed to do? I can't pressure her now....''

''Nobody said anything about pressuring her. And just because she isn't ready to marry you, it doesn't mean you can't be a part of her life. Just be there for her. Take care of her. Baby her. Before she knows it, she won't be able to imagine how she ever got along without you.''

The bell on the front door rang then with the arrival of the first patient. Within minutes the waiting room was filling up and there was no time for anything but work. But all morning long, as Lucas treated colds and flu and bronchitis, Mary's advice rumbled around in his head, nagging him, distracting him with images of ways he could pamper Rocky. By noon, he knew what he was going to do.

Morning sickness. Rocky had barely climbed out of bed when it came out of nowhere to send her rushing to the bathroom, where she had, to put it bluntly, tossed her cookies. After that, she hadn't dared touch breakfast. She knew she had to eat— the baby needed it—but her stomach seemed to turn over just at the thought of her putting food in it. So lunchtime came and went and she still put off going into town to the café for something hot.

"You go ahead," she told Charlie, who usually went with her to lunch. "I don't think I want anything."

Pulling on his jacket, he shoved his hands into his pockets and studied her suspiciously. "You okay? You haven't said two words since you got here, and then you looked like death warmed over. Something wrong?"

"Not a thing." Deliberately avoiding his too-sharp gaze, she kept her attention on the ad she'd been working on all morning, which she wanted to place in a popular hunting magazine. She knew she would have to tell him sooner or later about the baby, but she wasn't up to it now. As chauvinistic as Lucas, he would probably agree that she had no business flying, and that wasn't an argument she was ready to repeat anytime soon. "I had a big breakfast," she fibbed. "I'll get something later. Go on. I'll hold down the fort."

He went, but not without warning her that he was bringing her back some chicken soup—any day she didn't eat, she had to be sick as a dog, and if she wouldn't look after herself, then he would. Rocky was still smiling over his gruff concern when the door slammed shut behind him.

When it opened again almost immediately, she looked up, ready to tease him about worrying over her worse than a mother hen. But the tall, broad-shouldered man filling the doorway to her office wasn't Charlie. It was Lucas. And with a will of its own, her heart jumped into a crazy rhythm at the sight of him.

Irritated, she turned her attention back to the ad, though she couldn't for the life of her have said what it said. "If you've come to pick up where we left off last night, you've wasted your time," she said coolly, without sparing him a glance. "My answer is no, and it's going to stay no."

She braced for an argument that never materialized. Instead, he said easily, "Whatever you say. Have you had lunch?"

"No, but—"

"Good, because I packed us a picnic."

"A picnic? Are you kidding? It's freezing outside!"

"Then we'll eat in here." Setting a wicker picnic basket on the chair angled in front of her desk, he opened it and pulled out a red gingham table cloth. "Give me a hand with this, will you? We don't want to mess up the stuff on your desk. What are you working on, anyway?"

He didn't give her time to think, let alone answer, and in the time it took for her to remember that she didn't want to put so much as a drop of water in her sensitive stomach, he had a complete picnic—with everything from paper plates and potato salad to fried chicken—set up on her desk. The smell of the food alone would have been enough to tempt the devil himself.

Her mouth watering in spite of the memory of that morning's dry heaves, she eyed the little scene warily. Just who did he think he was fooling? He hadn't given up on convincing her to marry him— he was just trying another tactic. Now he was go-

ing to try seducing her into what he wanted, and she
wanted no part of it. Or him.

But, Lord, that chicken smelled good!

"I'm not hungry," she said hoarsely.

"You sure? I've got all sorts of tasty stuff here.
You like pickled beets?"

She loved anything sweet-and-sour, but she had
no intention of telling him that. Narrowing her eyes
at him, she said, "I know what you're doing and
it's not going to work."

He didn't deny he was up to something, but simply shrugged easily. "Okay, you caught me. But
you still have to eat. Try a bite." Scooping a beet
out of a decorative jar with a small plastic fork, he
held it up to her mouth and grinned down into her
eyes. "C'mon, just a little one."

With that wicked, heated gaze of his, he could
have charmed her into venturing out on a tight rope
without a net. Damn the man, why did he have to
be so attractive? Fighting a smile, she opened her
mouth.

The tartness of the beet exploded on her tongue,
drawing a soft moan from her. She saw Lucas's grin
deepen and punched him in the shoulder. "Damn
you, Lucas. If I get sick again—"

"So that's why you didn't want to eat, huh?" he
murmured as he trailed a finger over the curve of

her cheek. "Morning sickness? Why didn't you say so?"

She stared up into his eyes, her pulse fluttering at his touch. It was all she could do to hang on to the topic of conversation. She wanted to lean into his touch, into him, and lose herself in him. Instead, she forced herself to pull back just the slightest bit, until he was no longer touching her. It helped, but not much. "Because I don't even want to think about it," she said huskily. "It was awful. Can I have some more of those beets?"

He laughed and slung a friendly arm around her shoulders to steer her around her desk to the chair behind it. "You can have anything you want. Sit down, and I'll fix you a plate."

She should have protested. She had a feeling that when Lucas was at his most charming, he could be impossible to resist, but suddenly she was starving. And what harm could it do to share a meal with him? He could ask until the cows came home, but she wasn't going to marry him. All she had to do was remember that, and they'd get along just fine.

Settling back, prepared to enjoy a rare moment of being pampered, she watched him fill her plate with all sorts of tempting morsels. "Where'd you get all this stuff? And don't tell me you made it yourself because I won't believe you. You're probably all thumbs in the kitchen."

"I'll have you know I can cook a mean steak," he retorted as he set her plate before her, then began to fix one for himself. "Just don't ask me to try anything more complicated than that. Most of this came from the deli at Thompson's store in town. You like it?"

Taking a bite of a deviled egg, Rocky closed her eyes and savored it, the corners of her mouth curling in a satisfied smile. "Mmm... I love it. I can't remember the last time I was on a picnic."

"I can," he said as he dragged up a chair across from her and proceeded to dig into his food like a field hand. "I was in med school, and it was the middle of summer. One of my friends set me up with a blind date—a nursing student whose main goal in life was to marry a doctor. Of course, I didn't know that, but my friend did. We'd hardly set the food out before she launched herself at me and sent us both tumbling into an ant bed."

"Oh, no!" Rocky choked, trying not to laugh. "That must have been awful. What'd you do?"

"Rushed her to the hospital—she was allergic."

"To you or the ants?"

"Cute, Rocky," he said, grinning. "To the ants, of course. But she was so embarrassed after that that whenever she happened to run into me on campus, she ducked around the corner like I had the plague or something. Needless to say, we never went out on another date."

"The poor girl probably wanted to crawl into a hole. Did she ever get herself a doctor?"

Laughter danced in his eyes, wicked and enticing. "Yeah. John—the friend who set up the blind date—ended up falling for her like a ton of bricks. Last I heard, they had three kids and were expecting a fourth. He's working all the time just to feed them and set up college funds for all of them."

Fascinated by this side of him, Rocky couldn't help but laugh. "And just think—it could have been you."

He nodded, grinning. "There but for the grace of God and those ants." Leaning across the desk, he added another egg to her plate. "Here. Have some more."

"Lucas! I'm going to be as big as the side of a barn if you keep that up."

She was laughing when she said it, but it was the wrong thing to say. His eyes took a slow, lazy inventory of her curves, noting the fullness of her breasts beneath the navy turtleneck sweater she wore, the smallness of her waist, the flare of her hips. He didn't touch her, but he didn't have to. Between one heartbeat and the next, she was hot and breathless, and they were both remembering that night in the mountains when they hadn't been able to get enough of each other.

"Maybe John has the right idea," he said thickly. "You're going to be a beautiful expectant mother. Your skin already has a rosy glow."

The color in her cheeks was nothing but an old-fashioned blush, but Rocky couldn't find the words to tell him. Her pulse was thundering, her blood was warm, and the dark, secret recesses of her body were pulsing from the memory of his loving. She should have been horrified, but all she could think of was that they were alone and all she had to do was reach out her hand and he would take it. Her fingers itched just at the thought.

The sudden ringing of the phone was like a scream in the heated silence, shattering the tension. She jumped, the hot color in her cheeks turning a fiery red. Lord, she hadn't blushed so much since she was a teenager! What was the matter with her?

Fumbling for the phone under the tablecloth, she snatched it up with fingers that weren't anywhere near steady. "Fortune Flying Service," she said shakily, avoiding Lucas's penetrating gaze. "This is Rocky. May I help you?"

"I certainly hope so, baby sister," her brother drawled in her ear. "How're things going?"

"Adam!" Delighted, she asked him to hang on a minute, then told Luke, "I'm sorry. It's my brother, and I haven't talked to him in ages. I've got to take it."

"No problem," he said, pushing to his feet with the animal grace that never failed to draw her eye. "I need to check with Mary to make sure everything's quiet at the clinic. Is there another phone around?"

"On Charlie's desk, out in the work area," she said. "Just punch 9." He thoughtfully shut the door behind him, and she quickly turned her attention back to her brother. "Everything's fine here. How're the kids?"

"Holy terrors," he retorted with a chuckle. "God knows how I'm going to control them when they hit their teens. They can scare off a baby-sitter faster than any kids I've ever seen. But that's not why I called."

Something in his tone had alarm bells going off in her head. Ever since their grandmother had died in that Brazilian rain forest, it seemed like the family had hardly dealt with one crisis before another one hit. Dragging in a calming breath, she braced for the worst. "What is it this time? Another break-in at the lab?"

"Not quite," he said tersely, then dropped the bombshell. "Dad's decided to sell some of the family's stock to Monica."

"*What?*"

"I know. It blows the mind, doesn't it? She's already bought up everything she can get her hands on, and now for some reason, Dad's selling her even more."

"Mother must be livid," Rocky said, frowning. "Aside from the family, Monica's already the majority stockholder. If she gets her hands on enough shares, Dad might as well hand her the keys to the front door. Maybe you should talk to him."

"Me? You've got to be kidding."

Rocky winced at her brother's caustic tone and wished there was something she could say to make his relationship with their father easier. But they were both strong, opinionated men who didn't see eye to eye on hardly anything. Consequently, they'd been alienated for years, and a reconciliation was nowhere in sight. It was positively infuriating.

Still, Rocky had never been able to resist the need to play peacemaker. "If you'd just cut him a little slack—"

"Why should I? He never has me."

"But—"

"Save it, sis," he growled. "I'll never have a relationship with him like you and Allie and Caro. There's just too much water under the bridge."

It didn't have to be that way, but Rocky knew that tone. It was a carbon copy of their father's when he'd made up his mind that he wasn't going to budge another inch. Fighting a smile, she wondered why the two men couldn't realize they were just alike. But there was no sense in trying to convince Adam of that. He would never believe it.

"I know you're not going to want to hear this," she said, "but we're just going to have to trust Dad on this. It's not as if he's going to do anything to hurt the company. He lives and breathes for it just like Granddad Ben did—which is why Kate left him in charge. And he does own his own shares outright. He can sell them to whoever he wants to and there's nothing we can do about it."

"Except consider having him committed," he retorted, "because he's obviously lost his mind."

Rocky laughed—she didn't know anyone more in control of his mental facilities than their father. Whatever reason he had for doing this, it wasn't because he was a couple of bricks shy of a load. "Mother might not be speaking to him right now, but somehow I can't see her doing that," she replied in a voice laced with amusement.

Changing the subject by mutual consent, they spent the rest of the call talking about Rocky's new flying service and what was going on with the rest of the family. She didn't tell him about the baby— she wasn't ready for the questions that would bring down upon her head—and when she hung up a few minutes later with a promise to keep in touch, she was smiling. But that didn't last long. What could have possessed her father to sell shares to Monica?

"Problems?"

Lost in her musings, she blinked and looked up to find Lucas peering around her office door. She forced a smile, but it was obviously strained. "Nothing that I can't handle. Come on in. Everything okay at the clinic?"

"Yeah. The after-lunch crowd will be arriving soon, but I've still got a few minutes." Leaving the door open, he strode across to her desk and sank into the chair he'd occupied earlier, his sharp eyes immediately noting how she stared distractedly down at the food that only moments ago had tempted her. Cursing the phone call that had destroyed the mood between them, he tried to tell himself that whatever now had her in a blue funk was none of his business—but it was his business when she didn't eat. And that affected his baby.

Frowning, he asked bluntly, "Did your brother call with bad news?"

"What?"

"The phone call," he said, prodding her. "Was it bad news? You seem to be off on another planet."

She hesitated, then shrugged, her smile crooked. "Sorry. You know how family is—they call you about things you've got no control over, then leave you to stew on it all day. It's nothing. I hope," she added under her breath.

"You know, I've been told I'm a damn good listener. If you need someone to talk to, I'm all ears. Sometimes it helps to dump it on someone else."

With a will of their own, her eyes dropped to his shoulders. They were broad and strong enough to shoulder any burden. A woman could confide in a man with shoulders like that, a man who could wrap an arm around her and make the world go away. Given the chance, she might have laid her head against his chest and told him anything.

Before she could stop herself, she said, "My father has agreed to sell more shares in Fortune Cosmetics to Monica Malone."

He arched a dark brow in surprise and whistled softly. "Seems like I read something about her a while back, in the business section. Isn't she already the largest nonfamily stockholder? And your father's selling her some of the family's holdings? Is that wise?"

"No, but there doesn't appear to be any reasoning with him. Adam's furious. He can't understand what's gotten into him, and Dad's not talking."

"Does your father usually explain his decisions to the family?"

"No, but we could lose the company over this one."

"If he sells enough to give Monica a controlling interest," he pointed out. "Do you really think he'd do that?"

No. She didn't even have to think about that. Jake might be infuriating at times, but he was as sharp as a scalpel when it came to business. And he despised Monica Malone. There was no way he'd hand the company over to her on a platter.

"No," she said, giving him a relieved smile. "Of course not. I don't know what I was thinking of. I guess Adam just caught me by surprise."

"From what I've heard about your father, he'll still be wheeling and dealing when he's in his nineties," Lucas said dryly. "I don't think you have anything to worry about."

Rocky felt the same way, but just hearing him say it made her feel better. And that bothered her more than she cared to admit. He was an easy man to talk to, to confide in, and she couldn't make the mistake of turning to him for emotional support every time she felt the need. Because there was no future for the two of them. Not now. Not ever.

Eight

It seemed Lucas had barely left to return to the clinic before he was back again. Going over the Cessna to make sure everything was in order before she took up a real estate broker and his client, who were interested in checking out a nearby ranch that was for sale, Rocky didn't even notice him until she turned around and almost tripped over him.

Surprised, she could do nothing to stop the quick smile of pleasure that sprang to her lips. "What are you doing here? I thought you had patients this afternoon."

"Only a few—just the usual colds and flu. I heard you were going up and thought I'd go along...if you've got room for an extra passenger."

Puzzled, Rocky couldn't believe he was serious. "Well, of course we've got room, but this isn't a medical emergency. And what about the clinic? Shouldn't you be there in case you're needed?"

"I won't be completely out of touch," he assured her. "You've got a radio on board. Mary can call Charlie if anything comes up, and he can notify us."

He had it all worked out. And the more Rocky thought about it, the more she didn't like the sound of it. She was a firm believer in coincidence, but his showing up here by chance just when she was in the middle of a preflight check and getting ready to go up was just a little too pat for her to swallow.

Her dark brows knitting into a frown, she checked to make sure her customers were out of earshot, then asked suspiciously, "How'd you know I had paying customers? I didn't know it myself until they showed up here fifteen minutes ago, wanting to charter the Cessna."

He shrugged—and avoided her searching gaze. "Just lucky, I guess."

"Lucky my aunt Fanny," she retorted. "It was Charlie, wasn't it? He called you, didn't he? Just wait till I get my hands on him—"

"Hold it," Luke growled, grabbing her arm before she could hunt the older man down and read him the riot act. "This was my idea, not Charlie's, so don't go raking him over the coals for something I did. I asked him to call me every time you got a call to fly so I could go along to make sure nothing happened to you."

Touched, yet indignant over his high-handedness, Rocky wanted to believe his overprotectiveness stemmed from true caring. But he'd never mentioned how he felt about her, and she was afraid this was just a need on his part to control her.

Disappointed and alarmed—when had she started to need him to care?—she shook off his hold. "I won't have you interfering in my life this way," she grumbled. "I don't care what kind of a deal you made with Charlie, I don't need a baby-sitter when I fly. I'm perfectly capable of taking care of myself, so you might as well go on back to your clinic. The answer is no. You're not going up with us."

"Then I'll just have to tell those two dudes over there that you're pregnant and get vertigo when you fly," he snapped. "Before you know it, the word'll get around town and you won't be able to pay a customer to go up with you."

"You wouldn't dare!"

"Watch me."

They stood toe-to-toe, nose-to-nose, glaring at each other like two kids in a schoolyard. If she wasn't so furious, Rocky would have laughed. But there was nothing comical about his threat. He would do it. She only had to look in those hard, determined eyes of his to know that he meant what he said. With a few well-chosen words, he could completely ruin her business before it ever got off the ground. Literally.

"That's blackmail," she said stiffly.

He shrugged, unconcerned. "So sue me."

"Don't push me, Doc. For two cents, I just might do that."

"Go ahead, sweetheart, and see how far it gets you. No jury in this country is going to condemn a man for looking out for the welfare of his unborn child and its mother."

He was right, and she knew it. "Damn you, Lucas, I'm pregnant, not sick! You don't have to hover around me like I'm going to collapse any second. I'm as healthy as a horse."

Sensing victory, he grinned. "I'm glad to hear it. I'd hate for the pilot to lose her lunch while we're up in the air. When do we take off?"

Beaten, secretly welcoming his company, she had no choice but to give in as graciously as she could manage. "*We* are leaving in about fifteen minutes. And I guess there's room for you to go along. *This* time. But don't think you're going to get in the habit of following me around like a watch dog," she warned. "It's not going to happen."

"Whatever you say, honey," he said with an innocence that didn't fool her for a second. "I aim to please."

She snorted at that and went back to her pre-flight check, leaving him to introduce himself to the other two passengers, which he had no trouble doing. Within minutes, the three men were laughing and talking like old friends, which, for some perverse reason, irritated her no end. What was so funny, anyway?

Finishing the last-minute check and finding everything in order, she sighed, releasing the tension in her jaw, and forced a smile as she turned to face her customers. "Okay, gentlemen, we're ready to go. You can board now. Mr. Haggendorf, why don't you take the passenger seat in the front, so you can see better?" she suggested, since he was the buyer interested in the ranch they would be flying over. "If you'll take the seat behind him, Mr. Smith," she added to the Realtor, "you can point out items of interest." That left the seat directly behind her for Luke.

He took it without a word of complaint, and within seconds, everyone was buckled in and she had the Cessna racing down the runway. It was a cold day, but perfect for flying. There wasn't a cloud in the sky, and the winds were light. Ordinarily Rocky would have lost herself in the freedom of it, but all her attention was focused on Lucas. Even though he carried on an easy conversation with the other two men, she could feel his eyes on her, watching her every move. Just as if she were going to toss her cookies any second, she thought in growing resentment. And what would he do if she did? Take the controls? Not bloody likely!

Automatically circling the property Mr. Haggendorf was interested in so that he could get a better look at it, she silently cursed herself for knuckling under to Lucas's little blackmailing scheme. She'd wimped out, she thought in disgust, steaming. Just like she had with Greg. Except with Greg, she'd given in most of the time just to keep the peace. With Lucas, she'd really wanted him with her. And for no other reason than that, she should have called his bluff, dammit. Just because she was carrying his baby didn't mean he had the right to push his way into her life. And she was going to tell him so just as soon as they landed and she got him to herself.

Mr. Haggendorf, however, was in no mood to land anytime soon. Instead of just inspecting one ranch, he and the Realtor had a whole list they wanted to inspect from the air, and Rocky could hardly complain since they were paying very well for the service. It took hours, and not once over the course of the afternoon did Charlie radio her that Lucas was needed back at the clinic. By the time she returned all three men to the landing field, she was tired, her back was hurting her, and it seemed to take all her energy just to summon a smile when Richard Smith, the Realtor, paid her and promised to call on her again whenever he had someone interested in the large ranches in the area.

"I can be ready to go within an hour's notice," she promised him as she handed him a receipt for payment. "Just give me a call."

Lucas, hovering protectively by her side, noticed the shadows under her eyes and said quietly as soon as they were alone, "Are you okay? You look a little tired."

It was obviously the wrong thing to say. "Don't start with me, Doc," she growled, whirling on him like a tornado. "You're damn right I'm tired. My back hurts, I feel like I haven't eaten in a week, and I'm so mad at you I'd like to string you up by your toes."

"Me?" he squeaked innocently. "What'd I do?"

"Don't give me that wide-eyed little-boy look. You know exactly what you did. And I'm not going to put up with it. Do you hear me?" she demanded, punching him in the chest. "You can't wrap me in cotton and set me on a shelf like I'm some kind of china doll. I didn't let Greg do that, and I won't let you—"

"Greg," he cut in tersely. "So that's the bastard's name. I was wondering. So what did he do to you?"

She rolled her eyes in exasperation, wanting to shake him. "See? There you go again. I don't need you to fight my battles for me. I handled the jerk all by myself, and I can handle you."

"You can try, honey," he agreed soothingly, fighting a smile. Capturing her hand against his chest, Lucas wisely decided not to argue with her. But it was damn difficult when he thought of her handling any man but himself. God, where was this damn jealousy coming from?

"I'm not your honey," she grumbled as she struggled to free her hand, then gave up in defeat and left it where it was against his heart. "You have no rights at all where I'm concerned."

"Not a one," he agreed, lying through his teeth. "C'mon, sweetheart, it's just about quitting time. Why don't I take you home—"

"I can't. I have to help Charlie close up shop for the night."

"No, you don't," the mechanic growled from the open door of her office. "I'm not so old that I can't do it by myself every once in a while, and you look like a whipped puppy. Go home and put your feet up before you fall on your face."

She hesitated, and Lucas could practically see the struggle going on inside her. Lord, she hated showing weakness, especially in front of him. He'd never met her grandmother Kate, but he had a feeling she was a lot like her. Strong and independent and stubborn as a cuss. Why had he never realized before how much he liked that in a woman?

"What's it going to be, Rock?" he asked softly. "The call's yours."

She shouldn't. She had responsibilities, and she couldn't put them off on Charlie just because she was tired. But just the thought of sitting down somewhere and putting her feet up sounded like heaven.

Before she could stop herself, she heard herself tell Charlie, "Tomorrow you can leave early, and I'll do the closing up."

"The hell I will," he growled. "You can close up for me the day I'm pregnant, and not until then. Now go on with you," he scolded, shooing her toward the door. "I've got work to do."

"You heard the man," Lucas chuckled. Grabbing her coat from the old-fashioned hat rack standing in the corner, he hustled her into it. "Time to go home. Where are your keys?"

"Here," she said, and pulled them from her pocket.

Lucas promptly snatched them from her hand. "I'll drive. And don't give me any lip about it, Miss Independence," he warned when she opened her mouth to protest. "I know you can take care of yourself and do anything a man can and more, but just humor me tonight, okay? Just this once? *Please?*"

When he looked at her like that, she could no more resist him than a compass could resist magnetic North. Lord, she was in trouble. Feeling her resistance start to melt, she gave him a stern look. "All right. Just for tonight. But this isn't going to become a habit, Lucas."

"I totally agree," he fibbed, steering her out of the hangar and over to where her car was parked on the south side of the building. "Next time you get to baby me."

She laughed. He was teasing, of course, but there was nothing funny about the tantalizing images that stirred to life in her head. All too easily, she could see herself catering to his every whim, pampering him—not because she had to or he expected it, but because she wanted to. Because he was just as solicitous of her. Because she was beginning to care much more than she should.

Her heart pounding at the thought, she let him bundle her into her car, fasten her seat belt and drive her home without a word of protest. The next time she looked up from the fantasy which was becoming more and more appealing, they were parked in her driveway and he was patiently holding the passenger door for her, his eyes dark and searching as he watched her.

"Oh!" Hot color firing her cheeks, she fumbled for the release to her seat belt. "I'm sorry. I hadn't noticed.... I mean, I was daydreaming—uh, vegging out. I guess I'm more tired than I thought."

"No problem," he said with a knowing smile. "You look like you could use a hot bath. C'mon in, and I'll run you one."

She should have protested, but the words just wouldn't come. So while she collected her gown and robe, Lucas started the water in the old-fashioned claw-foot tub, poured in her favorite bath oil and lit candles.

Stopping at the sight of the seductive scene he'd created, Rocky felt her heart start to pound. The bathroom looked like something out of a dream. It was already growing dark outside, but he'd switched off the overhead light, leaving the candles to create a warm glow. Steam rose from the tub, and on the air floated the low, mellow sounds of one of her favorite Tony Bennett tapes. Surprised—how had he known?—she looked around and found her cassette player on the vanity.

"I found it in the kitchen," he said, following her gaze. "I thought the music might help you relax."

Relax? She almost choked as her nerves tightened in anticipation. How could she relax when she wasn't quite sure why he was here? "Lucas, this is all very nice of you—"

"But you don't need my help from here on out," he finished for her, grinning. "Don't worry, I wasn't going to offer to scrub your back. Maybe next time." Catching her off guard, he leaned down and brushed her mouth with his. "Take your time," he said huskily. "I'll scrounge around in the kitchen and see what I can whip us up for supper. Holler if you need anything."

He was gone before she could get her thundering heart back under control, quietly shutting the door behind him. Staring after him at the closed door, Rocky drew in a deep, settling breath. If this was his idea of pampering, she might be in trouble. Because from what she had seen so far, it was definitely something she could get used to.

Later, she had no idea how long she'd stayed in the tub. Immersed up to her shoulders in the steaming, fragrant water, she felt the tension seep out of her tired bones and laid her head back against the rim of the tub with a contented sigh. With her eyes closed and Tony Bennett crooning in her ear, she might have lain there for hours. But then the water began to cool. She stirred and caught the scent of something fabulous coming from the kitchen. Just that quickly, she was ravenous.

Hurriedly pulling the drain plug, she stepped from the water and she was reaching for a towel just when Lucas knocked at the bathroom door.

"Rocky? How's it coming in there? Supper's just about ready. You need some help?"

"No!" Her heart in her throat, she jerked the towel around her dripping body and told herself not to be a fool. He couldn't see through the door, and if he'd intended to walk in on her, he wouldn't have stopped to knock. And it wasn't as if he'd never seen her naked. Still, her voice was shaky when she told him, "I . . . I'll be right there. Just give me a minute to get dressed."

"No problem. I'll start putting the food on the table."

He walked away without another word, his footsteps loud in the hushed silence as he returned to the kitchen. Letting her breath out in a rush, Rocky realized she'd never be able to take a bath again without picturing him there, in her bathroom, lighting candles for her and running the water, kissing her. Why, dear God, had she ever agreed to this? He was carving a niche for himself in her life, and she was letting him. It had to stop.

She would talk to him, she promised herself, and lay down the law. Just because she was carrying his baby, that didn't mean that he had the right to anything where she was concerned. Somehow, she would get that through to him. But after supper, she decided as her stomach grumbled, reminding her that it had been hours since she'd had lunch. First she had to eat.

Luke was damn proud of himself. Giving the table a critical eye, he thought it didn't look half-bad, considering what he'd had to work with. Whatever else Rocky was, she obviously wasn't much of a cook. Oh, she had expensive cookware and a set of dishes that had probably cost the earth, but her freezer was practically bare except for frozen pizzas and TV dinners. And there wasn't a cookbook in the place. He wasn't much of a gourmet himself, but he drew the line at TV dinners. Digging a can of stew out of the pantry, he'd topped it with a package of canned biscuits he'd found in the refrigerator, then stolen some candles from the living room to decorate the kitchen table. He might have the knives and forks in the wrong place, but he was willing to bet that stew tasted damn good.

"Something smells wonderful."

At Rocky's husky greeting, he turned, ready to tease her about her eating habits, but the second his eyes found her standing in the doorway from the hall, the words stuck in his throat. Her face bare of makeup and her hair still damp and curling from her bath, she wore a flannel gown and a robe and foam booties. Lucas's eyes told him there was nothing the least bit sexy about the getup, but other parts of his body disagreed. His gut clenched, and suddenly just breathing normally was a chore. Soft and mussed and slightly rumpled, she looked as if she'd just crawled out of bed.

Stop right there, a voice in his head warned sternly at the thought. *Don't even think about hauling her off to bed. You're here to give her a little TLC, nothing else. You try seducing her and you could lose whatever slim chance you've got of talking her into marrying you.*

It was good advice, but just remembering what it was like to make love to her made concentrating on anything else damn difficult. God, she had him tied in knots! And that scent she wore didn't help matters. Soft and subtle, it floated over to him and teased his senses, wrapping around him until all he could think of was her...the taste, the feel, the warmth of her.

His smile tight, he said thickly, "It's just canned stew. Have a seat while I get us something to drink."

He turned away while he still could, but there was nowhere to run. After pouring them both glasses of milk, he had no choice but to take the seat opposite her. Under the table, his foot accidentally nudged hers, and he felt heat streak up his leg like a bolt of lightning, straight to his loins. Muttering a curse, he jerked his foot back as if he'd been scalded.

If Rocky noticed, she gave no sign of it, but calmly proceeded to serve herself and chatter about how relaxed she felt after her bath. Feeling as if someone had connected electrical wires to his nerve endings, Lucas could only envy her. The way he felt right now, he'd never be able to relax again.

They both dug in, but any chance Luke had of enjoying the meal had gone up in smoke the second she stepped into the kitchen doorway. The stew tasted like mush, the milk seemed to thicken in his throat, and the only appetite he had was for her. Sometimes life could be a real bitch.

By the time he'd cleaned his plate, his only thought was to get out of there. He needed some time to himself to figure out what the hell the woman had done to him. But when Rocky rose to her feet to carry their plates to the sink, she winced slightly and pressed a hand to her back.

"Your back's hurting you again?"

"Yeah," she sighed. "I guess it's something I'm just going to have to get used to." Rubbing at the aching spot, she grimaced.

He should have left her to deal with the problem the best way she could—after all, she'd made it clear that she didn't want him in her life—but he couldn't walk away. Not yet. Taking the plates from her, he set them back down on the table and grabbed her hand. "C'mon. I'll give you a back rub."

"Oh, but you don't need to do that—"

"Yes, sweetheart, I do," he said grimly, finding her bedroom and tugging her into it. She just didn't know how much he needed to get his hands on her. Just for a second, he promised himself. What could it hurt? "Kick your shoes off and stretch out on your stomach," he said in a rough voice as he stopped next to her antique oak bed and turned her to face it. "I'll have you feeling better in no time."

"But you probably need to be going. What if one of your patients needs you?"

"Mary will beep me," he assured her. "Quit worrying. Unless, of course, you want me to leave. I know you've had a long day—"

"No! Don't go!" The plea popped out before she even had an inkling it was there. Horrified, she slapped her hand over her mouth, but it was too late to take the revealing words back. Her cheeks stinging with hot color, she could do nothing but try to dog-paddle out of water that was suddenly over her head.

"I mean . . . it's not that late, and I'll be fine as soon as I get horizontal. I just need—"

He cut in gently. "I know what you need. Lie down, Rocky. Let me take care of you, honey."

When he spoke like that, in that deep, tender voice that seemed to rumble up from his soul, her will just melted. Without a word, she kicked off her shoes, grabbed her pillow and lay down.

She felt the bed dip as he sat down beside her, and should have tensed, but she was just too exhausted. Then his hands settled on her shoulders, kneading gently, and she couldn't have stiffened if her life depended on it. It—*he*—felt wonderful. Sure, knowing, talented, his fingers worked at muscles that seemed to have been knotted forever, smoothing out the kinks one by one as they moved slowly, steadily, down her spine. By the time he reached her lower back, she felt as if she'd died and gone to heaven. Unable to hold back a low moan, she went boneless.

"That's it, baby. Just close your eyes and relax," he murmured, leaning over her to press a kiss to the shell of her ear. "I'll take care of everything."

With a sigh of contentment, she did as he asked, and the world slipped away to the nether regions of her consciousness. Time must have passed, but she never noticed. There was nothing but the feel of his hands on her, the magic of his fingers, the steady beating of her own heart in her ears as he turned his attention from her lower back to every muscle in her arms and hands to the soles of her feet. As spineless as a jellyfish, she loved it.

When he brushed a kiss over the arch of her foot, she giggled. Then he pressed his mouth to the inside of her ankle and lingered, his tongue teasing the sensitive skin there, and her giggle became a muffled groan. He touched her nowhere else, just there on her ankle, but suddenly every nerve ending in her body was tingling. "Lucas—"

He heard the faint protest in the husky calling of his name...and the sudden breathlessness of rising passion. He knew he should concentrate on the former and stop right there, but it was the latter that urged him on and that he found impossible to resist. His own blood was on fire and had been from the first moment he touched her. And, God help him, he didn't want to stop there. Not when she was soft and pliant on the bed and the memory of that night they'd shared on the mountain was suddenly there between them, as tempting as the devil himself.

Still, he couldn't take advantage of her and risk destroying the fragile trust they'd managed to find over the past few hours. His fingers unconsciously tightening on her ankle, he said hoarsely, "I know. I feel it, too, honey. You know I want you—I can't seem to help myself when you're this close—but this has to be your call. If I keep touching you, I'm not going to be able to keep from making love to you. If that's not what you want, say so now.''

Bracing for rejection, he wondered how the hell he was ever going to find the strength to walk away from her, but instead of telling him he'd better leave, she rolled onto her side and reached for his hand. Without a word, she tugged him down on the bed beside her.

A slow smile curved the corners of his mouth as his eyes met hers. ''Does this mean you don't want me to leave?''

For an answer, she lifted a delicately arched brow. ''What do you think?''

What he thought was that he was going to die if he didn't have her, and damn soon. How long had it been since he'd kissed her? Really kissed her, and lost himself in the taste and feel and wet, giving heat of her mouth? Days? Weeks? A groan of need rising in his throat, he leaned over and pressed his mouth to hers.

He promised himself he was going to take this slow and easy. He wanted her wild for him and hot, so much in need that she wouldn't even remember her own name when he finally put them both out of their misery and took her. But the second his lips touched hers, her arms came around him, and it was like coming home. His thoughts blurred, his heart thundered in time with hers, and she gave him back kiss for kiss, touch for touch, as if they had been lovers for an eternity and had done this hundreds of times before, instead of just once.

Trust. It was there in the way she arched under his hands as he tugged her robe and gown from her, in the way she cried out when he moved over her, dropping kisses over every sweet, naked inch of her. It was his name she called, his shoulders she clung to as if she would never let him go. Touched, emotion gripping his heart, he felt her move against him, her hips nudge his, and the control he'd been so sure was unshakable was suddenly very shaky indeed.

His teeth gritting on a groan, he reminded himself that she was pregnant—he couldn't take her like a madman. But she murmured his name and kissed him long and sweetly, and it was all he could do just to hang on to his sanity. A muscle ticking in his jaw, he tried to tell her that he was close to losing it. "Sweetheart . . . I don't want to hurt you—"

"But you are," she murmured huskily, nipping at his ear as she moved her fingers to the snap of his jeans. "I ache, Doc. Can't you do something to make it feel better?"

He closed his eyes on a groan. "God, sweetheart, don't do this to me. . . ."

"What? This?" Through his jeans, she dared to caress him, and found him hard and ready for her.

Lightning-quick, his hand closed around hers, but the damage was already done. She knew he wanted her more than he wanted his next breath, and there was no stopping her. The rasp of his zipper was loud in the expectant silence, and then she was pulling his clothes from him and he was helping her.

After that, there was no time for talking, no time for anything but hot, openmouthed kisses and hands that seemed to never stop moving. Her breath caught in her lungs, her heart quickened, and he shuddered as her fingers curled into his hips. Then his hands were parting her legs, his fingers gently searching, and the world could have stopped without either of them noticing.

Urgency flared between them and burned like a flame in their blood. Her legs circled his hips, and with a low groan he surged into her. In the dim light that spilled into the bedroom from the hall, her eyes met his. Then there was nothing, nothing but the two of them moving together, racing toward the sun.

Nine

"Marry me, sweetheart. Let me take care of you and the baby. You know we belong together."

Snuggled spoonlike in the darkness, his chest pressed to her back and his arms cradling her to him, Lucas murmured the proposal in her ear like a temptation and had no idea how much Rocky wanted to jump at it. She loved him. She'd been fighting the truth for weeks now, but after tonight, when she felt more content and safer than she ever had in her life, she could no longer continue to deny the love that burned in her heart. He was a good man—honest and caring—and he would make a wonderful father and husband. All she had to do was say yes.

God, how she wanted to! The word was right there on the tip of her tongue, but before she could get it out, the arm around her waist tightened, pulling her more firmly against him, and he said huskily, "We can make it work, honey. I know you have doubts and you don't want to give up flying right now, but in your heart, you've got to know it's the right thing to do. And just because you give it up for now, it doesn't mean you'd be grounded forever. After the baby comes, we'll talk about it.''

Just that easily, the moment was shattered. Hurt, disillusioned, she could just imagine how they would talk about it. He would decide that the mother of his child had no business flying all over the wild blue yonder when she had a baby to take care of, and that would be that. End of discussion.

Sudden tears stinging her eyes, she threw off his arm and scrambled out of bed before he could stop her. ''What's the use of talking about it?'' she asked bitterly as she snatched up her robe and struggled into it. ''You're never going to approve of me flying, so the answer is no. I can't marry a man who doesn't support what I do.''

His jaw granite-hard, he snapped on the light. ''Why do you have to be so damn stubborn about this? I never said I didn't support what you want to do. But it's different now, dammit! You're pregnant, and you've got a baby to think about.'' Tossing back the covers, he rose naked from the bed, magnificently male and furious as he jerked on his jeans.

''I do think about it,'' she said angrily. ''That's why I can't marry you. You want a traditional wife who stays home where she belongs and doesn't take risks. That's not me, Lucas, and it never will be, so you might as well get used to it. I'm going to continue to fly as long as I can—"

"Just to prove to me that you can."

"No, dammit! Because it's what I do. What I've always wanted to do. I'm sorry if that upsets you, but it's really none of your business."

"The hell it's not!" he growled. "In case you've forgotten, that's my baby you're carrying. And whether you like it or not, that gives me a whole hell of a lot of rights where you're concerned. If you won't take care of yourself, I will."

She lifted her chin at that, refusing to flinch at the fury that rolled off him in waves. "You can't do anything I don't allow you to do, and no one's going to stop me from flying. Not right now."

They glared at each other like two fighters in the ring, neither willing to back down, the tension in the air so strong it practically crackled. Frustrated, so angry he wanted to throw something, Lucas muttered and cursed and jerked up his shirt from the floor. Trying not to think about how it had gotten there, he pushed aside the image of her tugging at his clothes until he'd been as naked as she and said grimly, "That doesn't mean I'm going to stop trying, so you might as well get used to it. Every time you even think about taking one of those damn planes up, I'm going to do whatever I have to to keep you on the ground."

Bristling, she demanded, "Are you threatening me?"

"You're damn right I am," he said curtly, heading for the door. "And if you don't like it, tough. I protect what's mine."

What was *his!* she fumed, sputtering. Oh, she'd tell him what was his—nothing, that was what! She wasn't a commodity to be owned, dammit! But before she could open her mouth to tell him just that, he was gone, slamming the front door so hard that the windows rattled.

She winced and only then remembered that he'd driven her home in her car. And as furious as she was with him, she couldn't let him walk home in the dark when it was freezing outside. Jerking open the front door, she half expected to find him waiting on the porch, fighting the need to ask her for a ride home. Instead, he was backing out of the driveway in *her* car!

"Hey!"

"I'll bring it back tomorrow," he yelled through the open driver's window. "You're not going to need it, anyway. You're not going to work."

"The hell I'm not! Damn you, Lucas, you come back here! Do you hear me?"

For an answer, he only waved jauntily and drove off. If she could have gotten her hands on him, she would have killed him.

*   *   *

The snowstorm hit just before dawn, whistling and moaning like something straight out of the bowels of hell, and it was still going strong two hours later, when Rocky was ready to go to work. And she *was* going, she assured herself grimly. She didn't care what Lucas said or how long he kept her car. It was in just such conditions that her services were needed the most, and she planned to be right there by the phone if a call came in. If that meant calling the sheriff's office for a ride so that she could get there, then so be it.

But just as she glanced out the living room window to see how deep the drifts were, Lucas drove up in his Bronco. Surprised—after his parting shot last night, she hadn't expected to see him at all today— she moved to the front door, the light of battle gleaming in her eyes as she waited for him to knock. If he was back to pick up where they'd left off last night, she was ready.

But the knock she waited for never came. Instead, she heard a thud near the back porch, then another. Puzzled, she headed for the kitchen and opened the back door just as another thud shook the back porch. Blowing snow swirled inside on a brisk north wind, hitting her in the face, momentarily blinding her, but not before she saw Lucas unloading a cord of firewood into the woodbox on her back porch.

Stunned, she quickly wiped the snow from her eyes and stared, a slow smile starting to curl the corners of her mouth. He was still more than a little miffed with her—she could see it in the rock-hard set of his jaw—but that hadn't stopped him making sure she stayed warm in what promised to be the first blizzard of the season. Some men brought roses, others jewelry. Lucas brought firewood, even when he wanted to throttle her. And she loved him for it.

He glanced up and saw her then, saw her smile, and his jaw relaxed slightly. "Go on back inside before you catch cold," he said gruffly. "I'll be in as soon as I finish this."

It didn't take him long—maybe fifteen minutes—but by the time he stepped through the back door into the kitchen, he was covered with snow. She took one look at him and hurried to the bathroom for some towels. "You didn't have to do that," she said as she brushed the snow off his head and shoulders. "Especially during a blizzard. Are you okay?"

He shook himself like a giant bear, sending the last flakes clinging to his hair and coat flying. "Yeah. Just a little damp around the edges. I brought you something."

"Yes, I know, and I appreciate it, but—"

"Not the firewood," he cut in. "This." Holding up a familiar white paper **bag,** he waited expectantly for her reaction. He didn't have to wait long.

Her eyes wide, she looked at the sack as if it held the treasures of the pyramids. "You brought me doughnuts from Pop's?"

"Yep. I heard you liked the double-dipped chocolate ones."

She didn't have to ask where he'd heard it. Pop's Bakery was an institution in Clear Springs that Rocky had discovered soon after she moved there. Jim Stanwick, known to everyone as Pop, made every conceivable kind of doughnut known to man, each one guaranteed to melt in your mouth. But it was the double-dipped chocolate ones that Rocky just might have sold her soul for. And Pop knew it.

Grinning, Rocky started to reach for the bag, only to jerk her hand back as if she'd been burned. Suddenly suspicious, she eyed him warily. "This is a bribe, isn't it? You give me the doughnuts and I'm supposed to agree to stay home today, right?"

"It's a peace offering, honey. Nothing more. God knows I'd feel better if you wouldn't go anywhere today, but I'm not holding my breath. Charlie already caught a ride to my place and drove your car over to the airfield for you. I'll take you there when you're ready to go."

Unable to believe he was serious, she searched his face for some sign that this was a trick, but she'd never seen him more serious. A lesser woman would have gloated over the victory, but something warm and sweet expanded like hot air in her heart, and suddenly she couldn't seem to stop smiling. Peaking inside the bag of doughnuts, she lifted impish eyes to his. "All of these are for me?"

"Well, I was sort of hoping you'd share a few with the father of your baby. But if you really feel you can't spare any, I've got another bag out in the car."

She burst out laughing. "You dog! You'll take mine and keep yours for yourself?"

"You're damn right," he said, grinning. "A man's got to look out for himself. So am I invited for breakfast or not?"

It would serve him right if she sent him away, the rogue, but she didn't have the heart. She'd had a miserable night last night, and she hated the angry words they'd traded. She wasn't foolish enough to believe he'd changed his mind about her continuing to fly, but he'd obviously accepted the fact that he couldn't change the situation, and for that she could have kissed him. Instead, she asked teasingly, "Would you like to stay for breakfast, Doc? I seem to have more doughnuts than I can possibly eat."

Grinning, he shrugged out of his coat and pulled out a chair at the kitchen table. "I thought you'd never ask. Have you got any coffee?"

The day went downhill from there. Lucas gave her a ride to the airfield, as promised, only to get an emergency call just as he pulled up before the hangar. Giving her a swift kiss, he promised to call her later, then drove away as fast as the hazardous road conditions would allow. Two hours later, she heard from him. He'd been flooded with calls from patients who couldn't make it into the office, so he was going to spend the rest of the day making house calls. Staring out her office window, Rocky told herself that he'd grown up here—he could no doubt handle whatever Mother Nature threw at him. But as the hours passed and the storm continued to worsen, she couldn't help but worry.

By late afternoon, an unnaturally early twilight had fallen. The snow hadn't let up for a minute, and the roads were impassable. Nothing short of a four-wheel-drive vehicle was going anywhere without a tow truck. And more snow was expected throughout the night.

Rocky had been waiting all day, pacing restlessly, for some sort of emergency call. It came at a quarter to five, just when she was giving serious consideration to locking up shop and going home.

"Fortune Flying Service," she said into the phone, after snatching it up on the first ring. "May I help you?"

"I certainly hope so," Sheriff Alan Nighthawk growled. Identifying himself, he said, "I just got a call on three hikers lost on the south rim of the mountains. I need you to help find them."

It wasn't a request, but a demand, one that Rocky didn't even consider bucking. Not when three people were stuck on the side of a mountain somewhere and didn't have a chance of surviving the night without her help. "Are any of them injured? Where were they last reported to be? How familiar are they with the area?"

She threw one question after another at him, and the answers he gave her weren't good. The hikers were teenagers and new to the area. They'd started out right after breakfast for Devil's Canyon, one of the most dangerous areas on the south face of the nearby mountains, and hadn't taken anything but a lunch and their down jackets. They should have been home hours ago. When they hadn't shown up within a reasonable time, their families had gone looking for them, but without success. Worried sick, they'd called the sheriff. Not only was it getting dark, but one of the boys had asthma and had forgotten to take his inhaler with him.

It couldn't, Rocky decided, have been much worse. "Give me ten minutes to fuel up the chopper and get some supplies together, and I'll be on my way," she told the sheriff. "I'll keep in touch through the radio."

Before she'd even hung up, she was yelling for Charlie. Hurriedly explaining the situation to him, she grabbed blankets and food and enough first-aid supplies to take care of an army. "There's no time to lose," she yelled over the whistling moan of the wind as he rolled open the hangar door and she got a good look at the sky. "It'll be dark in an hour, and if we don't find them before then, there won't be much point in looking for those kids until spring. You got her all gassed up?"

"Yeah, but I don't like the looks of that sky," he hollered back as the skullcap he wore went flying. "Things start icing up and you could be in real trouble. Maybe you should tell the sheriff to find somebody else."

"There is no one else," she reminded him. "Not unless he can get someone from Jackson, and even then, it would be dark before they could get here. I've got to go, Charlie. Those kids are depending on me."

He didn't like it, but there wasn't much fault he could find with her reasoning. "All right, dammit to hell, but you be careful! You hear me? If anything happens to you, the doc'll string me up by my toes and leave me to dry. Get on with you, before it gets any darker.''

Grinning, she gave him a thumbs-up signal and helped him get the chopper out of the hangar. Seconds later, she was preparing for takeoff when the passenger door was suddenly jerked open and she looked over to find Lucas scowling at her with eyes that were nearly black with fury. "Lucas, what—?''

"Have you lost your mind?'' he thundered. "Shut that thing down right now, or so help me, God, I'll shut it down myself.''

"I can't. Dammit, Lucas, don't you dare come in here and tell me how to run my business at a time like this! I've got three kids lost in the mountains, and if I don't find them within the hour, they'll have to spend the night up there. I don't have to tell you what their chances are of making it until morning. So either get in or out, but do something. I've got to go.''

He got in, but only because he wasn't going to take a chance on letting her fly out of there before he could talk some sense into her. He'd been halfway across the county when he heard about the kids on the radio, and every instinct he had had warned him the sheriff would call her in on the rescue effort. He'd broken all speed records getting to her. When he drove up and saw her already in the cockpit and revving the motor, his heart had stopped in his chest.

"Let Charlie go," he said tersely. "I'll go with him, and you can stay here. Dammit, Rocky, you're pregnant!"

"Nothing's going to happen to me or the baby," she assured him. "Believe me, if Charlie could do this for me, I'd let him, but he can't. He doesn't have the training for mountain rescues. It's either me or nobody." Her eyes, dark and earnest, locked with his. "Lucas, those are somebody's kids. What if one of them was ours?"

It was a low blow, one that came out of nowhere to tug at his heartstrings. Their baby, nearly grown up, a teenager full of sass and suddenly in trouble. The images that played before his mind's eye left his throat dry and his heart pounding. He couldn't even imagine how he would feel if there was only one person who could help his child and that one person refused. Rocky was right—she had to go.

Frustrated, wanting to throw something, he spit out a curse and reached for the seat belt. This was madness, pure insanity. He was needed at the hospital to help handle the emergencies that were flooding in, but there were other doctors in town who could take his place. There was no way in hell he was letting Rocky fly off in a blizzard alone. "Let's go."

Buckled up, their headphones in place so that they could communicate with each other over the roar of the rotors, they took off seconds later and headed straight for the mountains in the distance. Or at least where they knew the mountains to be. With the steadily falling snow and the thick gray clouds that clung to the peaks, concealing them from view, it was nearly impossible to see the rocky range in the gathering gloom until they were almost upon it. And then what they saw was hardly encouraging.

The south face of the mountains looked like an arctic wasteland. There was nothing but wind and snow and ice. Drifts had covered craggy canyons and concealed sudden drop-offs. Rocky stared through the blowing snow where she knew a particularly hazardous hiking trail to be and felt her stomach fall away at the thought of a bunch of unwary kids coming that way. They wouldn't stand a chance.

"See anything?" Lucas asked over the sudden sick thudding of her heart.

"No, but the visibility stinks. I'm going to go in closer."

"Just be careful," he growled, never taking his eyes from the snow-covered ground below. "This wind's a bitch."

Her jaw clenching until it ached, she slowly took the chopper as low as she dared, her gaze, like Lucas's, trained on the icy terrain below. There was no sign of life anywhere. "Maybe they didn't make it this high up the mountain," she said hopefully. "Once they saw how bad it was, they might have found shelter at the campground at Spring Lake. There's no one there this time of year, but there's an old cabin nearby. Let's check it out."

It took only a few minutes to fly to the lower elevation and find the frozen lake which was a favorite hangout for teenagers in the summer, but it quickly became apparent that if the three boys had headed there, they'd never made it. The lake was frozen and deserted, the campground empty. The cabin, nearly lost in the drifts that had piled up around it, wouldn't be much use to anyone in the near future. Snow had piled up on the roof and caved it in.

Hovering over it, staring down at the broken timbers that poked up through the snow, Rocky searched the immediate area for tracks, but there weren't any. "They're not in there," she said firmly, not sure who she was trying to convince— Lucas or herself. "They can't be. They would have tried to light a fire. And there would have been tracks. . . ."

Tracks that would have long since been covered up by the blowing snow, Lucas thought privately, examining the scene below for any sign that anyone had been there recently. But there was none. Like Rocky, he had to believe that if the boys were there, they would have at least started a fire to keep from freezing to death.

"They might not have even come this way," he replied. "The hiking trail splits halfway up. The east fork leads to the lake, the west to Eagle's Nest Canyon. There's a cave there."

Without a word, Rocky headed west, just skimming the treetops as the already poor light began to fade. Tension, hot and needling, clawed at her nerve endings as she felt time slipping through her fingers. If the boys weren't at the cave, they wouldn't be found tonight. There just wasn't enough time to look anywhere else before it became completely dark and flying conditions worsened.

But the cave, they soon discovered, like the cabin, was completely deserted.

"They're not here, Rocky," Luke said grimly, breaking the tense silence. "If they were, they would have come running the second they heard the chopper. The weather's getting worse. We need to head back."

"No!" She knew he was right, but all she could think of was that she and Lucas were those three boys' last hope of being found alive. If they gave up on them, they would have no one. "Just a few more minutes," she pleaded. "It's not completely dark yet."

If the situation had been the least bit humorous, Lucas would have laughed at that. It was so dark that he had to strain just to see her in the light from the instrument panel. Unless the boys had flares, which they had no reason to believe they did, picking them off the side of the mountain in the dark would be nearly impossible.

"I don't like giving up on them, either, honey," he said gruffly. "But the wind's picking up. And that looks like ice on the windshield. We've got to get the hell out of here while we still can."

The radio crackled to life then, startling them both. Snatching up the transmitter, Rocky said, "This is Fortune One. Come in, Sheriff."

"We found them, Rocky. On the other side of the mountain. They just called in. They're all safe— just a little shook up and worried about what their parents are going to do to them."

At his chuckle, Rocky grinned. "If they were mine, I'd ground them for life. Thanks for the call, Sheriff. We're heading back now. Over and out."

"Thank God!" Lucas sighed. "Now we can get the hell out of here. I don't like flying so close to the trees."

Considering the conditions, Rocky wasn't too fond of it herself, and she immediately tried to increase altitude, but the chopper only lurched and threatened to stall out. Her heart stumbling in her breast, she tightened her grip on the throttle. "Damn! Ice must have built up on the rotors. Maybe I can shake it loose."

She tried, but it quickly became apparent that she was fighting a losing battle in the quickly deteriorating weather conditions. The snow that had been falling all day was now mixed with sleet, icing everything in sight as the temperature steadily dropped. The rotor blades couldn't take much more and still keep them in the air.

"I'm going to have to find a place to set her down," she said around the lump of sick panic that lodged in her throat. "Now!"

The words were hardly out of her mouth when they suddenly ran out of time. The rotor blades slowed, causing the chopper to lurch sideways. Then they were falling, crashing through the trees, breaking them. Someone screamed—Rocky never recognized the sound as coming from her own throat—and then the gnarled limb of an old pine shattered the windshield and slammed into her like the jagged edge of a rusty knife. She gasped, struggling to hold on to consciousness, but darkness descend with terrifying swiftness. Before she could do anything but whimper, she was swallowed whole by the night.

Seconds, an eternity, after they started to lose altitude, the chopper slid to a bone-jarring stop at the base of an old pine. From high in its lofty limbs, snow shook loose and tumbled down onto the wreckage, spilling into the cockpit through the shattered windshield in a nearly soundless puff. The wreckage settled and groaned, and then there was nothing. Nothing but silence and the mournful sound of the wind.

Lucas came to to find himself slumped against the passenger door, his teeth clamped on an oath and his hands clutching at the sides of his seat as if it were a lifeline. Dazed, he realized he must have hit his head and blacked out for a few seconds, but he had no memory of it. In fact, the last thing he remembered was the tree crashing through the windshield and Rocky's soft moan—

"Oh, God! Rocky? Sweetheart?" Jerking upright, he turned toward her and stopped dead at the sight of her pinned to her seat by a broken tree limb that pierced her side. Barely breathing, as white as the snow that filtered through the broken windshield, she was unconscious and covered in her own blood.

For a split second, he couldn't move, couldn't do anything but freeze as the past rose up like a specter in front of him. With agonizing clarity, he saw Jan lying broken and bleeding on the rocks at the bottom of the sheer cliff she'd fallen from, dying before his eyes. "No!"

Later, he didn't remember fighting his way out of his seatbelt or cursing the tree limbs that filled the front of the cockpit as he struggled to reach her. Once again, the life of the woman he loved was in his hands, only this time, dear God, he wasn't going to lose her. "Hang on, honey," he told her in a choked voice, feeling for her pulse. "You hear me? Just hang on."

If she heard him, she gave no sign of it. Her pulse was steady, but growing weaker by the second. And the blood . . . God, she'd lost so much! He had to stop the bleeding.

But when he bent to inspect her side and got a good look at the wound for the first time, his fingers weren't quite steady. The branch, which was a good two inches in diameter, had splintered off from the main tree when they crashed into it, but what was left was firmly embedded in Rocky's side, just under her rib cage. If he pulled it out now, she'd bleed to death before he could even find his medical bag in the wreckage.

He had to operate.

Emotion seized him by the throat, denial twisting in his gut, but there was no avoiding the inevitable. She was losing blood steadily. If she was going to live to see the sunrise, he had to do something and do it now.

The decision made, he reached for the radio mike and called for help, citing their approximate location, even though he wasn't sure the sheriff or anyone else heard him. When he waited for a response, all he got was static. "Damn!"

Slamming the transmitter down, he found some flares under Rocky's seat and stuffed his pockets with enough to completely encircle the helicopter's wreckage. He didn't light them, though, until he was sure there wasn't a fuel leak anywhere. If anyone came within sight of the old abandoned cabin, which the sheriff knew was their last known destination, they wouldn't be able to miss the crash site. It was lit up like a birthday cake.

After that, there was nothing left to do but carry Rocky to the back of the helicopter and carefully lay her down on one of the stretchers that she always carried for emergencies. He'd found his medical bag buried under the rubble that had once been the cockpit and sent up a silent prayer of thanks that he kept it well stocked. In spite of that, he knew it was going to take all his skill, plus help from the man upstairs, to pull off a major operation under what could only be described as the most primitive of conditions. It was cold and dark and far from sterile—he didn't even want to think about the infection she was going to get from that damn tree. But that was something they could deal with later. First he had to save her.

"You're going to make it, honey," he told her fiercely as he positioned the flashlight he'd found with her emergency supplies. "Do you hear me? I'm right here, and I'm not going to let anything happen to you."

She moaned, but didn't regain consciousness, which was probably a blessing in disguise. All he had to deaden the pain was a local anesthetic. It would help, but if she woke up, she would be in agony. Washing his hands in rubbing alcohol, which was the only disinfectant he had, he set out everything he could possibly need, then reached for the tree limb, knowing that the second he pulled it out there would be no time to lose.

"Don't die. Don't die. Please, dear God, don't let her die."

The prayer falling like a litany from his tongue, he drew in a bracing breath and pulled the limb from her torn flesh.

Ten

What followed was like something out of one of his worst nightmares. The wind whistled through the broken windshield of the chopper, blowing snow everywhere, and the flashlight beam seemed to grow weaker and weaker. Cursing, he bent closer to Rocky's still body and tried to hurry, praying that she wouldn't wake up before he finished. But his fingers were numb and clumsy from the cold, and he had to stop every few minutes and blow on them just so that he had feeling in them. And with every tick of the clock, time seemed to be running out.

His brow damp with the sweat of worry, his concentration focused on finding all the bleeding veins, he never heard the mumbled prayers that fell from his own lips. He made God outrageous promises, pleaded with him, and begged. A proud man with a proud heritage, he begged as he had never begged in his life. And when he was finally finished and the last bleeder was found and repaired, the torn skin stitched, there was nothing else he could do but wait.

It was the longest night of his life.

Her vital signs were strong, but when she didn't regain consciousness, the worry eating at his gut like a cancer intensified a thousand times. She was so still. And white as death. He packed the thermal blankets around them both and hovered close to keep her warm, but still, she didn't waken. His eyes never leaving her face, he stretched out beside her and went over the operation again and again in his head. If he'd missed one bleeder, which would have been easy to do with the poor lighting, she could be in trouble.

That thought alone kept him awake for what seemed like hours. He heard every moan of the wind, every creak of the helicopter wreckage as the weight of the falling snow built up outside. By morning, they would be completely covered and nearly impossible to spot from the air if the flares ran out. But that was something he couldn't worry about now. Now his only concern was getting Rocky through the night.

Considering that, he shouldn't have been able to sleep a wink. But exhaustion caught up with him sometime after midnight, numbing his mind and weighting his eyelids until he could no longer keep them open. But even in sleep, he didn't relax his guard where Rocky was concerned. On some unconscious level, he was aware of her beside him, the warmth of her under the covers, the slow, steady rhythm of her breathing. And when she stirred, shifting ever so slightly, he was instantly awake and on his knees beside her, his fingers finding the pulse in her wrist before he'd even blinked the sleep from his eyes.

"Rocky? Sweetheart? Can you hear me?"

She moaned—it was a low groan that was nearly lost in the wailing of the wind—her face etched in furrows of pain as she moved restlessly, searching for a position that was free of pain. But there was none, and with a weak sigh, she finally went still, giving up the fight. Cursing his inability to do any more for her than he already had, Lucas leaned over her and pressed his stethoscope first to her heart, which was strong, then to her abdomen. In his ears, the baby's heartbeat was faint, but steady. Relief washed through him like a flood, bringing a thick clog of emotion to his throat. They were both going to be okay. They had to be! Nothing else was acceptable.

He started to draw back then, but he'd only moved a fraction of an inch when she moved suddenly, covering his hand and stethoscope with her fingers, trapping them against the warm skin of her belly. In the dim light provided by the rapidly fading flashlight, her eyes met his.

"The baby's fine," he assured her thickly.

She nodded, a bare whisper of a smile gliding across her dry lips as her fingers tightened around his. "I know," she whispered in a faint, husky voice that he had to lean closer to catch. "I knew you'd take care of us."

Her confidence in him, especially considering the circumstances, rocked him back on his heels. She was seriously injured, and it might be hours, possibly days, before a rescue team could find them. She had every right not only to panic, but to be worried sick about the baby. Instead, she closed her eyes on a sigh and drifted back to sleep, her hand still clutched around his as if she would never let him go.

Stunned, Lucas stared down at her and felt his heart turn over. God, she was something. And he loved her. More than he'd ever thought possible. Just the thought of her in pain tore him up, but she hadn't even mentioned it. If he could have, he would have wrapped her up in his arms and drawn her right inside his heart to protect her from harm, but all she needed was his hand in hers. And for now, that was all he could give her.

Stretching out beside her, his fingers still twined with hers, he lay there for hours, just watching her sleep and listening to the rhythm of her breathing. The flashlight batteries finally gave out. Then, one by one, the flares he'd set out right after they crashed sputtered out, making the darkness complete. He didn't want to leave her then, but he couldn't take the chance that their rescuers, when they finally got there, would fly over them in the dark and miss them. Quietly slipping away, he found more flares and set them out, cursing the cold that seemed to freeze the very blood in his veins, then hurried back to the helicopter and Rocky.

When the storm began to blow itself out, he couldn't have said. He must have fallen asleep, because he jerked awake abruptly, sometime near dawn to find himself curled around Rocky and a silence that seemed to scream echoing in his ears. A frown wrinkling his brow, he was trying to figure out what was wrong when it suddenly hit him that the wind had died. Finally, the storm had passed.

Sighing in relief, he glanced down at Rocky and frowned at the bright spots of color singeing her cheeks. Considering the cold, he wanted to believe that her heightened color was nothing more than windburn, but the second he laid his palm against her forehead and felt the heat rolling off her in waves, he cursed softly under his breath. She was running a temperature, and from the feel of it, it was sky-high. A slightly elevated temp wasn't that unusual right after surgery, but there was nothing slight about this, and it could mean only one thing—an infection.

She shifted restlessly under his hands, her eyes, weak and clouded with pain, fluttering open at his first touch. "Lucas?"

"I'm right here, honey. How are you feeling?"

"Like I went three rounds with a tree and the tree won," she joked faintly, shivering. "I have a fever, don't I?"

"Just a slight one," he lied, tucking the blankets closer around her after he gave her a shot of antibiotics to counter the infection running rampant through her. God, she was so pale! If she hadn't been flushed from the fever, she wouldn't have had any color in her face at all. "You'll be fine once I get you back to the hospital. Can I get you anything?"

Unable to keep her eyes open any longer, she let them close and sighed. "Just an electric blanket. Wake me when this is over. Okay?"

"You've got my word on it," he promised, but she didn't hear him. She'd already fallen asleep again.

Worried and no longer able to pretend to himself that she was going to be just fine, Lucas had never felt so helpless in his life. He'd missed something—he knew that now—but to go back in and open her up again, when his resources were limited and she'd lost so much blood, would leave her even weaker and put the baby at risk. Dammit, where was that rescue helicopter from Jackson? It should have found them hours ago.

Restless, unable to just sit there and watch her slip slowly away from him, he packed the covers around her, then moved to the cockpit of the chopper and grabbed the radio transmitter. The second he hit the power switch, it was obvious it was dead. Which meant the only hope they had of being found was his transmission of their location to the sheriff last night, he thought grimly. A transmission he wasn't even sure the other man had received because of the storm.

His gut clenched at the thought. "No, dammit," he muttered to himself. Even if the sheriff hadn't gotten the transmission, he'd known they were searching the south face of the mountains and they'd never made it back to Clear Springs. He would have already sent for help, and even now rescuers had to be searching for them. The only trouble was that he'd run out of flares hours ago, and with all the snow, the helicopter wreckage would be nearly invisible from the air. If he didn't do something, and damn fast, help could fly right over them and not even know it.

"A fire," he said suddenly. In the clear morning air and against the white background of snow, a fire would be visible for miles.

Hurrying outside, he grabbed some of the broken branches that still stuck through the shattered windshield and piled them up for a bonfire. The wood was green, however, and damp from the snow, and wouldn't burn without help. Swearing, he was digging in his medical bag for the bottle of alcohol he'd used last night to clean his hands when a faint, far-off droning sound seemed to set the air humming. At first, he hardly noticed. Then he heard it. A helicopter! The sound of its rotors carried easily on the clear, crisp air as it approached from the southeast.

He glanced up, searching for it, the beginnings of a broad smile of relief starting to stretch across his mouth. Then he finally found the chopper, just skimming the treetops on the horizon. If it keeps its present course, it would miss them by a good ten miles.

"No!" Swearing, he finally found the alcohol and snatched it up, reaching the pile of brush in three long strides. In less time than it took to draw several deep breaths, he'd doused the wood with the alcohol and struck one of the matches he'd found in the chopper's emergency supplies. With a low whoosh, the broken branches went up in flames, sending smoke climbing straight as an arrow into the air.

Time slowed to a stop. He never knew how long he stood there, staring at the chopper in the distance, fiercely willing its pilot to notice the smoke and come and investigate. But the helicopter continued farther to the east.

"No, dammit! This way! We're over here!"

His thunderous roar seemed to echo through the trees like the cry of a wounded bear. There was no way the pilot could have heard him, but the chopper suddenly lurched, almost hesitating in midair. Then it was racing right toward him. Sinking down on his knees in the snow, the fire crackling just a few feet away, Lucas sent up a silent prayer of thanks.

The pilot was a crackerjack sky jockey from Jackson who could have set the chopper down on a pinhead if the need arose. With his help, and that of the two paramedics he'd brought with him, they got Rocky loaded on a stretcher, put out the fire Lucas had started and had everyone back on board within ten minutes. A heartbeat later, they were racing for Clear Springs and the hospital.

The ride took twenty minutes. It seemed like an eternity. Worry clawing at him, Lucas hovered close to Rocky's side, murmuring to her to hang tough, but if she heard him, she gave no sign of it. Her face ashen, her body as hot as a furnace and her pulse too fast under his fingers, she lay unresponsive, totally unaware of her surroundings.

Then the pilot set the helicopter down right in the middle of the hospital parking lot, and the emergency room doctors and nurses came running. There was no time for goodbyes, no time for a kiss that might be their last, before she was being wheeled away. Staring after her, dread spilling through his bloodstream like a frozen arctic wind as he gave Roy MacDonald, the admitting physician, the details of the crash and the emergency surgery he'd had to perform, he watched the double doors of the emergency room swing shut on Rocky. Deep inside, he had the god-awful feeling that he was never going to see her again. And if he lost her, he had no one to blame but himself.

"Lucas?" Roy prodded when his words trailed off. "Are you okay? It looks like you took a pretty nasty blow to the head yourself. Maybe you should have it x-rayed."

Jerking back to attention, he said flatly, "I'm fine. Rocky's the one who's in trouble. I think I must have missed a bleeder. She's pregnant, Roy. If she loses the baby, she'll never forgive me."

"Now don't go talking that way," his friend growled. "She wouldn't have made it this far if you hadn't been with her, and you know it. So quit second-guessing yourself and go get yourself a cup of coffee while we check her out. You look like you could use it. I'll find you when we're finished."

He wanted to argue—wanted to say he wasn't going anywhere but into the examining room with Roy, to find out exactly what was wrong with Rocky—but he knew his friend was right. He was exhausted, on his last legs, his mind numb from worry and lack of sleep. He'd done all he could for her. It was time to let someone else take over.

He headed for the cafeteria and bought himself a cup of coffee that he couldn't get past his tight throat. Staring down at it, he stirred it until it was cold and didn't see Rocky's cousin, Kyle Fortune, and his wife, Samantha, hurry in until they were almost upon him. He didn't know them that well, only well enough to nod when he passed them in town, but they were the only family Rocky had in Wyoming, and he should have at least called them to let them know she was hurt.

Cursing himself, he got stiffly to his feet. "I'm sorry, Kyle. I should have called you. I just didn't think."

"We heard it on the radio," Kyle said. Pale under his tan, his hawkish features sharp with worry, he asked, "What happened? How is she? The nurse in the admitting room wouldn't tell us anything."

"They're still examining her." Offering them both chairs, he said, "You'd better sit down. This isn't going to be easy to hear."

He told them everything, from the moment they'd taken off in search of the missing hikers, to the seconds after the crash when he'd come to to find Rocky impaled on a branch and lying in her own blood. "I had to operate, or I would have lost her right there," he said huskily. "She'd lost so much blood, and there was no way to stop the bleeding with that damn tree stuck in her side—"

Samantha cut in quietly, her green eyes earnest as they met his. "You don't have to justify your actions to us, Dr. Greywolf. It sounds like you saved her life."

"We're just damn grateful you were there," Kyle added gruffly. "And I know the rest of the family will be, too, as soon as they hear about this. Especially Uncle Jake and Aunt Erica."

Lucas winced, guilt pulling at him. He was no knight, and the sooner they knew that, the better. "You might not be so grateful when you hear the rest of the story. Rocky's pregnant with my child."

He just blurted the words out with no finesse, then wanted to kick himself when he saw their start of surprise. "The baby's in no danger," he hurriedly assured them, "at least not so far. But Rocky's lost a lot of blood. Conditions weren't exactly sterile up there in the mountains for an operation, though, and she's developed an infection.''

Kyle, his deepset blue eyes narrowing unblinkingly on Lucas's face, said bluntly, ''Once she and the baby pull out of this, I presume you're getting married.''

It wasn't a question, but a demand, one that once would have been almost comical coming from a man like Kyle Fortune. He was a second son and a one time playboy, and it hadn't been all that long ago that he'd raced through life in fast cars bought with his family's money, avoiding responsibility and commitment as he went from one beautiful woman to another like a man who hadn't a care in the world. Then his grandmother had died, leaving him the family ranch outside of Clear Springs with the stipulation that he had to live there six months in order to inherit it free and clear. None of the locals had expected him to stay longer than a couple of weeks, let alone the full time, but then he'd met and fallen in love with Samantha Rawlings. Lucas had heard he was a changed man—apparently it was true.

''I asked Rocky to marry me,'' he said quietly, ''but she refused. She's got this crazy idea that I'm going to put a leash on her just because I'm concerned about her safety.'' Normally a private man where his feelings are concerned, especially with strangers, he couldn't seem to stop himself from telling them everything. "She's the stubbornest woman I've ever met in my life. I know she's trained with some of the best and she's an excellent pilot, but what she's doing is dangerous, dammit! She can't just go flying off around the countryside like she doesn't have a care in the world. She's got to quit being so reckless and think of the baby."

"*Caution* isn't a word that's ever been in my cousin's vocabulary," Kyle replied grimly, "but she would never do anything that would put her own baby or anyone else in danger."

"Not deliberately, no," Luke agreed. "But I can't risk losing her, dammit. I love her!"

Her green eyes dark with sympathy, Samantha pointed out softly, "There are no guarantees in life, Lucas. You must know that in your line of work. You could tie her to your side, watch every step she takes, and never let her out of your sight, and she could still get hurt in a car accident or struck by lightning. That's just fate. You can't try to make her into something she's not just because you're afraid of losing her."

She would have said more, but Roy MacDonald hurried into the cafeteria then and immediately started toward him. Bracing himself, Lucas rose quickly to his feet and introduced him to Rocky's cousins before saying grimly, "I missed a bleeder, didn't I?"

"You didn't miss anything except a sterile operating room," Roy retorted. "She's got a pretty bad infection, which is what you expected, but all things considered, you did a great job. Personally, I don't know how the hell you did it. There's no internal bleeding, and the baby's doing fine."

Stunned, Lucas could only stare at him. "Are you sure? She was so weak—"

Roy grinned and slapped him on the shoulder. "She's fine, Luke. I promise. She lost a lot of blood, but we're pumping her full of fluids and antibiotics, and she should be able to go home in a couple of days. If you don't believe me, go see her for yourself. She's in room 301."

His eyes searching Roy's, Lucas couldn't doubt his sincerity. She was going to be okay. And so was the baby. Relief swept through him like a rush of desert air, warming the cold, vulnerable hollows of his heart and lifting what felt like a boulder of worry from his shoulders. God, he loved her! It still stunned him how much. And he wouldn't, couldn't, lose her.

On some gut level, he'd known from the first moment his eyes met hers that she was going to turn his life upside down, and he'd been fighting it ever since. She could hurt him, could strip away the

barriers he'd built around his heart just by exist-
ing. And that scared the hell out of him. He didn't
want to be that vulnerable again, dammit. But he
loved her. In spite of the fact that she worried him
to death, he loved her gumption, her willingness to
go out in a blizzard to help three foolish teenagers
in trouble. And he wouldn't have had her any other
way.

Suddenly needing to tell her that more than he
had ever needed anything in his life, he started toward the cafeteria doors that led to the elevators.
Chuckling, Roy called after him, "Does this mean
you don't believe me?"

"No," Lucas retorted over his shoulder, grinning. "It means I need to ask the lady's forgive-
ness before I ask her to marry me . . . again."

Lying in bed in her hospital room, Rocky stared
out the window at the foot of new snow that had
fallen while she and Lucas were stuck in the mountains overnight. So close, she thought, shuddering.
They'd come so close to being killed. If the ice on
the rotor blades had been heavier. . . if the pines that
had shattered the windshield had struck her in the
abdomen instead . . . if Lucas hadn't been with her
at all . . .

God, she didn't even want to think about it! But
she couldn't bury her head in the sand and pretend

the past twenty-four hours hadn't happened. She— and the baby—were alive because of Lucas. If he hadn't insisted on going with her, she would have bled to death up there and would have had no one to blame but herself. She'd been so determined to find those hikers that she didn't think of the danger she was putting herself and the baby in, let alone what she was doing to the people who cared about her.

Pain gripped her heart, remorse bringing the sting of tears to her eyes just at the thought of Lucas operating on her. God, what kind of agony had she put him through? Because of her stubborn recklessness, he'd found himself in the untenable position of once again fighting to save the life of a woman he loved. And all the time he had to have been thinking of Jan and worrying that history was going to repeat itself.

Would he hate her for that? For foolishly putting herself at risk without a thought to what she might be doing to him or the baby? She had to see him, had to explain that this was all new to her. She hadn't loved anyone before, not the way she loved him. She hadn't expected to feel his pain as deeply as she felt her own, but just the thought of the torment he must have gone through when he pulled the branch out of her side and stitched her back together tore at her heart. What could she possibly say to make up for that?

Wondering where he was, wishing he was there so that she could explain, she'd never felt so miserable in her life. Sighing, she turned away from the window, leaned her head back against her pillow and closed her eyes. She never heard anyone come into her room, but when she felt familiar fingers wrap around her wrist to take her pulse, she realized she would have known that touch on the dark side of the moon.

"Lucas!" She looked up, found him standing right next to her, looking tired and worried and incredibly wonderful, and suddenly the words she hadn't been sure she'd be able to find were pouring out. "I'm sorry. You have every reason to be furious with me for being so stu—"

"No, I'm the one who should be apologizing. I've been acting like a Neanderthal—"

"I'm a daredevil. What can I say? Kate taught me everything I know. But I never meant to put the baby at risk. Or worry you to death. I just overreacted to your concern." She told him then about Greg, about his possessiveness, the hold he'd had on her that had scared her to death. "I was afraid of slipping back into that kind of relationship."

"I just didn't want to lose you. But that doesn't excuse trying to put chains on you. You know what you're doing—I know that. But just thinking about you getting hurt makes me crazy.''

''All I've been able to think about is the hell I put you through. I swear I won't do it again. Not if it means putting the baby at risk or taking stupid chances that are going to make you gray-headed before you're forty—''

''I don't want to change you. I know it must have looked that way, but I love you just the way you are—''

Each suddenly hearing the other, they both stopped in midsentence and simply stared at each other. Under his fingers, Lucas felt the jerk of her pulse. Then she was slipping her wrist free of his grip and grabbing his hand, holding on for dear life. With a groan, he sank down onto the side of the bed and reached for her, pulling her close. ''God, I love you so much!''

''I love you, too,'' she whispered huskily, burying her face against his neck. ''So much that it scares me.''

A rueful grin curled up the corners of his mouth. ''I know, honey,'' he said with a chuckle, tightening his arms around her. ''Believe me, I know. I was so afraid of losing you that all I could think of for the last few weeks was locking you up in my house and throwing away the key so nothing would happen to you. Do you think we could start over?''

She drew back, hope and love sparkling in her eyes like diamonds. "How?"

"By forgetting all the reasons why a marriage between the two of us couldn't possibly work and concentrating instead on all the reasons why it could. Like that I love your independence and your gumption and the way you don't let anybody talk you out of what you believe—"

"And I'm crazy about your protectiveness and the way you care about your patients and how even when you don't agree with what I'm doing, you're there for me—"

"I'll always be there for you," he promised, kissing her hungrily. "Either as your husband or your lover or both, for whatever you want to do. Whatever the future holds, we'll work it out together."

Her eyes searching his, she couldn't doubt his sincerity. He might not always agree with her, but his love and support were unconditional. Love flooding her heart, she lifted her mouth for another kiss and warned softly, "There'll be times when we'll fight. I can be bullheaded."

"I never noticed," he retorted, grinning. "I thought I was the one who could be stubborn as a mule."

"You are. God help this baby. I've got a feeling she's going to teach us both a thing or two about stubbornness."

Amused, he arched a brow at her. *"She?"*

She nodded. "The next one can be a boy."

Heat flashed in his eyes. "You're planning to have more children with me?"

Her smile was slow and sexy and loving as she slipped her arms around his neck. "I'm planning a lifetime with you, Lucas Greywolf. Didn't you know that?"

"I knew it the second I laid eyes on you," he growled, kissing her fiercely. "I just wasn't sure you did. Now that we've got that settled, what were you saying about more kids? I liked the sound of that."

Epilogue

"Kate, I'm not so sure this is a good idea," Sterling murmured worriedly in her ear. "The entire family is here! What if someone spots you?"

Her beautiful silver-streaked red hair concealed beneath an awful gray wig and a ill-fitting, deliberately frumpy wool dress that added pounds to her slim figure, Kate laughed merrily. "Don't be such a worrywart, Sterling. No one's going to notice me in this getup you insisted I wear. Not when the whole town's here. Anyway, I couldn't possibly miss Rocky and Luke's engagement party. Don't they look wonderful together? I've never seen Rocky so happy."

Peering through the boisterous crowd that filled the hangar at the airfield to overflowing, his own thick white hair covered with a harsh black rinse, Sterling had to agree. In the month since the accident in the mountains, Rocky had completely recovered from her ordeal and was positively glowing as she and Luke laughed and talked with Allie and Rafe. "She's beaming, Kate. Pregnancy and falling in love obviously agree with her. Did I tell you the rumor around the hospital is that they're planning a whole houseful of kids?''

She nodded, her throat tight with emotion. When they heard on the news that Rocky was recovering at the Clear Springs hospital after her helicopter had gone down in the mountains in a blizzard, she'd been worried sick until Sterling made a secret trip to the hospital to see for himself that she was okay. When he came back with the news that Rocky was not only okay, but pregnant and planning to marry Lucas Greywolf, she'd been thrilled. She'd wanted to rush to her side and hug her, to tell her how happy she was about the baby and her upcoming marriage to Luke, but that was out of the question until they discovered who was plotting to destroy the family and Kate in particular.

"They're going to make wonderful parents. And I plan to be part of their babies' lives,'' she warned Sterling. "I'm missing too much as it is. This standing-on-the-sidelines stuff is for the birds.''

Tall and dignified, even with that terrible color on his hair, Sterling only smiled. "I know, Kate. You never were the type to hang back in the crowd when you could be leading the pack, but you're going to have to be patient. We're getting closer to finding out who wants you dead, and in the meantime, it's not as if you've been totally cut off from the family. You haven't missed a single family event, and you're still safe. That's what's important."

She knew he was right, but still, it was hard. When she first let him talk her into staying *dead* until they discovered who her enemy was, she'd never dreamed it would drag on this long. And there was no end in sight. "You're right." She sighed. "I know you're right. I'm just being sentimental."

"It's one of your most endearing traits," he retorted, grinning. "And one of your most frustrating. You're not going to be content until the whole family's happy, are you?"

"Of course not. How can I be? And speaking of happy, Adam hasn't had too much to smile about for a long time now. We've got to see what we can do to help him."

"Oh, no, you don't," Sterling groaned, recognizing the glint in her eye all too easily. "You've already interfered in your grandchildren's lives enough. Adam doesn't need your help."

Far from discouraged, she only grinned. "Okay, I won't help him. We'll just give him a little nudge in the right direction.

"What do you mean ... *we?*" he asked suspiciously.

"Well, I can't do it alone," she said innocently. "I'm dead, remember? You'll just have to do it for me. Unless, of course, you want me to come out of hiding."

As he frowned down at her in pretended disapproval, it was all he could do not to grin. "You're a conniving woman, Kate Fortune."

Not the least bit offended, she laughed. "You ain't seen nothing yet."

"That," he groaned, getting in the last word, "is what I'm afraid of."

* * * * *

FORTUNE'S CHILDREN
continues with
SINGLE WITH CHILDREN
by Arlene James
Available in December
Here's an exciting preview . . .

Fortune's Children continues with

SINGLE WITH CHILDREN

by **Arlene James**

Available in December 1996

Here's an exciting sneak preview. . . .

Single With Children

"Is she gone?" Wendy whispered. Her freckled nose wrinkled in ill-disguised hope.

"She is." Adam Fortune's voice was resigned as he stared at his daughter.

"For good?" Robbie, Adam's middle child, looked up with little-boy innocence.

"Afraid so, thanks to you three."

Ryan, a slightly smaller version of his minutes-older brother, flashed a triumphant smile at Wendy before breaking into whoops of delight. Instantly the other two joined him, all attempts at regret abandoned.

"Gone! Gone! The witch is gone!"

Adam automatically assumed a military posture. "That's enough!" he barked in his most commanding voice—which used to scare his troops, but did nothing to his children. They were simply too delighted at having gotten rid of their latest nanny—the seventh in the past eighteen months.

Suddenly the children demanded breakfast. Adam gave a groan before he could help it. No one had even made coffee. Civilian life was hell.

He made a decision. He was good at decisions. In fact, deciding was what he did best, and this decision let him off the hook in several ways. For one thing, they'd actually eat, and for another, he wouldn't have to clean up the mess in the kitchen on an empty stomach. "All right, let's get you dressed. We're going out for pancakes."

Once again the children erupted. Adam smiled to himself. He might actually have scored some points with his kids with this one.

An hour later Adam asked himself how a good idea could have gone so wrong. He grabbed for the syrup pitcher yet again, snatching it out of the way as Robbie fell chest forward into his plate. Ryan immediately prepared to duplicate his brother's antics. "Oh, no, you don't!" Adam tried to catch Ryan, and succeeded in knocking coffee all over the place.

Then the pitcher was lifted out of his hand. An instant later it was replaced with a damp towel. "Allow me," said a soft voice. Adam caught a flash of uniform and a brown hair net as he wiped his thigh. He looked up in time to see a slender young woman tug Wendy's leg into place and situate the hand with the fork over her plate. She smiled at the girl, then put Ryan back into his booster seat. She leaned down and whispered something before moving on, and Ryan instantly began to eat. Robbie required a bit more attention.

"Well, now, handsome, you've made a mess of yourself, haven't you?" she said, ruffling his hair. "The food's supposed to go *in* your tummy, not on it." She dipped a napkin in his water glass and began dabbing the syrup off his shirt. Robbie grinned, clearly besotted, and Adam understood the sentiment as she turned the smile on him.

She was astonishingly lovely, with an oval face built of high, delicate cheekbones and a smooth forehead. Her straight, thick bangs were palest gold. Her lips were wide and perfectly shaped beneath a patrician nose. But her eyes dominated. Large ovals, they were a clear, brilliant green veined with blue and thickly fringed with tawny lashes.

"I think you've just averted a major disaster," he said. "Thank you."

She continued cleaning Robbie's shirt. "No problem." Her mouth quirked up at one corner. "You looked like you had your hands full."

Adam amazed himself with a warm chuckle. "Oh, yes. Our nanny just quit and I haven't gotten the hang of this single father bit, yet."

"Mommy's dead!" Ryan announced at the top of his lungs.

"My wife was killed eighteen months ago," Adam said softly.

"You poor darlings," she said, looping an arm around each of the twins' necks. She bent to kiss first Ryan and then Robbie and they soaked up her affection. She turned to Wendy. "You probably remember her well, don't you?" Wendy nodded. "I bet you miss her awfully, too." Wendy's lower lip trembled and the woman came around the table to hug Wendy.

"My heart just goes out to you all," she said, adding briskly, "Stop that right now, young man. We don't allow food to be thrown."

Just then a man appeared at her elbow. "Laura, you have customers waiting."

"Sorry, Mr. Murphy, I was just—"

"I told you," the man interrupted sternly, "no flirting with the customers!"

"But I wasn't—"

Adam cut in. "She was cleaning up after my son, when—"

The man pointed a finger to Adam. "I'll thank you to stay out of this. We have rules. You don't see the other girls batting their lashes at married men."

"He's not married!" Laura cried.

The manager smiled. "Not flirting, huh? You've already determined his marital status. I'm very disappointed in you, Laura."

Her mouth fell open. "The little boy said his mother was dead!"

Murphy glared at her. "I don't like argumentative employees. You have five seconds to get back to work or you're fired. Five. Four."

Adam rose. "This is absurd! She hasn't—"

"Three. Two."

"Don't bother!" Laura ripped off her hair net and freed a sleek cascade of hip-length blond hair. "I quit!"

"I knew you wouldn't last," the manager sneered.

Adam threw his napkin on the table. "Mister, you're asking for a broken nose!"

"No!" Laura interrupted. "I can't stand fighting. *Please.*"

Adam looked at her face and felt his heart lurch. He swallowed his anger. "Get your coats, kids," he ordered, digging into his pocket. "We're out of here. And we won't be back."

"What a tragedy," snarled the manager.

Adam fixed him with a narrow glare. "Tell your boss that he'll be hearing from Adam Fortune." Turning to the woman, he added, "I'll be out front when you're ready to go."

"One minute," she said, rushing away.

Adam gathered his kids to leave.

"Fortune?" The manager swallowed hard. "Uh...er...um... Breakfast is on the house, Mr. F-Fortune," he stuttered, trying to give Adam back his money. "It was just an, um, misunderstanding."

"Nice try," Adam said. "But I don't think so."

And as they left the restaurant, Wendy exclaimed, "I like her, Daddy! Don't you? Wouldn't she make a good nanny? Wouldn't she?"

"Yeah." Adam grinned at his daughter. "She might, at that."

* * * * *

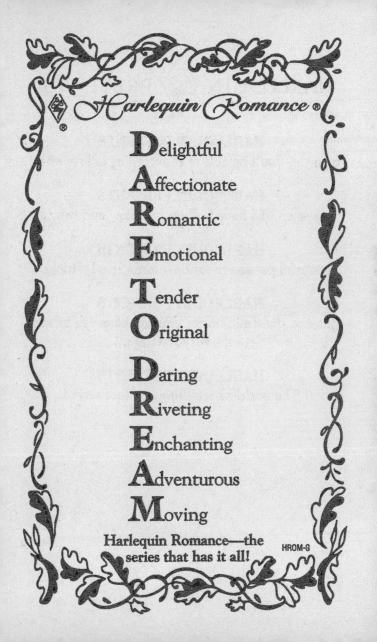

Harlequin Romance ®

Delightful

Affectionate

Romantic

Emotional

Tender

Original

Daring

Riveting

Enchanting

Adventurous

Moving

Harlequin Romance—the
series that has it all!

HROM-G

HARLEQUIN  PRESENTS®

HARLEQUIN PRESENTS
men you won't be able to resist falling in love with...

HARLEQUIN PRESENTS
women who have feelings just like your own...

HARLEQUIN PRESENTS
powerful passion in exotic international settings...

HARLEQUIN PRESENTS
intense, dramatic stories that will keep you turning
to the very last page...

HARLEQUIN PRESENTS
The world's bestselling romance series!

Harlequin® Historical

If you're a serious fan of historical romance,
then you're in luck!

Harlequin Historicals brings you
stories by bestselling authors, rising new stars
and talented first-timers.

Ruth Langan & Theresa Michaels
Mary McBride & Cheryl St.John
Margaret Moore & Merline Lovelace
Julie Tetel & Nina Beaumont
Susan Amarillas & Ana Seymour
Deborah Simmons & Linda Castle
Cassandra Austin & Emily French
Miranda Jarrett & Suzanne Barclay
DeLoras Scott & Laurie Grant...

You'll never run out of favorites.

Harlequin Historicals...they're too good to miss!

HARLEQUIN®

I N T R I G U E®

THAT'S INTRIGUE—DYNAMIC ROMANCE AT ITS BEST!

Harlequin Intrigue is now bringing you more—more men and mystery, more desire and danger. If you've been looking for thrilling tales of contemporary passion and sensuous love stories with taut, edge-of-the-seat suspense—then you'll *love* Harlequin Intrigue!

Every month, you'll meet four new heroes who are guaranteed to make your spine tingle and your pulse pound. With them you'll enter into the exciting world of Harlequin Intrigue—where your life is on the line and so is your heart!

Harlequin Intrigue—we'll leave you breathless!

LOOK FOR OUR FOUR FABULOUS MEN!

Each month some of today's bestselling authors bring
four new fabulous men to Harlequin American Romance.
Whether they're rebel ranchers, millionaire power brokers
or sexy single dads, they're all gallant princes—and
they're all ready to sweep you into lighthearted fantasies
and contemporary fairy tales where anything is possible
and where all your dreams come true!

You don't even have to make a wish...Harlequin American
Romance will grant your every desire!

Look for Harlequin American Romance wherever Harlequin
books are sold!

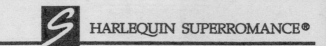
HARLEQUIN SUPERROMANCE®

...there's more to the story!

Superromance. A *big* satisfying read about unforgettable
characters. Each month we offer *four* very different
stories that range from family drama to adventure and
mystery, from highly emotional stories to romantic
comedies—and much more! Stories about people
you'll believe in and care about. Stories too
compelling to put down....

Our authors are among today's *best* romance writers.
You'll find familiar names and talented newcomers.
Many of them are award winners—and you'll see why!

If you want the biggest and best in romance fiction,
you'll get it from Superromance!
Available wherever Harlequin books are sold.